THE BLUE LINE LETTERS

PRAISE FOR THE BLUE LINE LETTERS

The Blue Line Letters takes readers on a wistful journey aboard Portland's famous MAX Blue Line. From nothing happening to a random cow hopping on, and from an unconventional prophet speaking the truth to a knife fight, *The Blue Line Letters* encapsulates a typical experience in one of America's weirdest cities. — Jason Tanamor, author of *Love, Dance, & Egg Rolls*.

Steven Christiansen's *The Blue Line Letters* is a lovely little homage to public transportation, to how reading and writing change the world, and to the Rose City itself. Ty Clark is an immensely sweet and touching protagonist in the style of Charlie from *The Perks of Being a Wallflower*, and his daily observations and wry insights endear him to the reader instantly. The brief, punchy chapters are often self-contained little gems of short stories and poetry, and supporting characters Omar and the Prophet are so compelling, you may hope they get their own spin-off sequels. It's a remarkable achievement to set a novel almost entirely within the confines of a MAX train car that somehow feels this free and breezy. YA maestro John Green would be proud of this novel. — Dean Backus, author of *Darts and Flowers*

Seventeen-year-olds live with surprises. Exhilaration and fumbles, comfort and queasiness, and the messiness of life all happen, usually without warning. Meet Ty Clark, who makes 50 round trips on MAX's Blue Line to and from his summer job, and writes their story for all of us to read.

Ty's fellow riders—the grouchy, the prophetic, the guys with knives, and the woman who gives birth between Old Town and Skidmore Fountain—are his human landscape, and standing out among them is the quietly intriguing Janie. Listen to Ty's evolving insights as he ponders great big questions because he has the opportunity to.

And there's a pair of otters, too.

How better to spend 100 MAX rides than practicing the fundamental, complicated, human art of paying attention? — Virginia Euwer Wolff, author of National Book Award winner *True Believer* and native Oregonian

The Blue Line Letters is a crackling-good adaptation of the epistolary novel. In revealing and introspective letters to his English teacher on his daily commute to a summer job, seventeen-year-old Ty invites readers into his world as he ponders (and complains about) *Jane Eyre*, life, school, and his very own Janie. Ty's witty and authentic voice will resonate with teen readers, as will his interactions with—and reactions to—the menagerie of people he observes every day on Portland's MAX Blue Line. One of the most engaging coming-of-age novels I've read in years, it's sure to be a hit with YA readers—and their teachers. — Chris Crowe, author and professor of English at Brigham Young University

THE BLUE LINE LETTERS

Steven Christiansen

Ooligan Press | Portland, Oregon

The Blue Line Letters
© 2025 Steven Christiansen

ISBN13: 978-19-47845-58-9

All rights reserved. No part of this book may be reproduced or transmitted in any form or by any means, electronic or mechanical, including photocopying, recording, or by any information storage and retrieval system, without permission in writing from the publisher.

Ooligan Press
Portland State University
Post Office Box 751, Portland, Oregon 97207
503.725.9748
ooligan@ooliganpress.pdx.edu
www.ooliganpress.com

Library of Congress Cataloging in Publication Data on file.

Cover design by Isabel Lemus Kristensen
Interior design by Ariana Espinoza

References to website URLs were accurate at the time of writing. Neither the author nor Ooligan Press is responsible for URLs that have changed or expired since the manuscript was prepared.
Printed in the United States of America

Library Writers Project

Ooligan Press and Multnomah County Library have created a unique partnership celebrating the Portland area's local authors. Each fall since 2015, Multnomah County Library has solicited submissions of self-published works of fiction by local authors to be added to its Library Writers Project ebook collection. Multnomah County Library and Ooligan Press have partnered to bring these previously ebook-only works to print. The Blue Line Letters is the fifth in an annual series of Library Writers Project books to be published by Ooligan Press. To learn more about the Library Writers Project, visit https://multcolib.org/library-writers-project.

Ooligan Press Library Writers Project Collection

The Blue Line Letters by Steven Christiansen (2025)
Court of Venom by Kristin Burchell (2022)
Finding the Vein by Jennifer Hanlon Wilde (2021)
Iditarod Nights by Cindy Hiday (2020)
The Gifts We Keep by Katie Grindeland (2019)

To Alisha

Cleveland Avenue, Day 1

Hey Ms. Warne,

Here goes nothing. Actually, it is something, but I couldn't figure out another way to start my assignment. Sorry for the cliché of, "Here goes nothing"—I know you think clichés are not good writing.

In case I don't make up a title page for this summer work, or if I don't put my name on it somewhere, I guess I'll just let you know that this is Ty Clark, your favorite student from third period last year. This will sound cheesy, but I'm glad you're "moving up" and will be my English teacher again next year. Although, I do have to say that your summer reading assignment is going to give me some serious grief. *Jane Eyre*? Seriously? Who still assigns students to read *Jane Eyre*? Is it like the only book the school has enough copies of to send home with us students over the summer? Nobody reads this book anymore, come on.

The only reason I'll read this lame book is because I'm trusting you on it. That book you had us read last summer turned out to be pretty cool, so I'm giving you the benefit of the doubt. Sorry—that was another cliché. I actually bought my own copy of *The Things They Carried* and even had my dad read it. He really liked it too. He's interested in Vietnam, and he reads a lot.

The other assignment you gave us—"What we learned over the summer"—seems a bit second grade-ish, but since it's not going to be hard to do, I won't complain, even if it sounds like I am complaining right now.

You might have noticed the title of my first chapter or entry: Cleveland Avenue. It's the first (or last) stop of the MAX Blue Line. You probably already know that. My mom has some connections and got me a paid internship for the summer. She said to me, "Ty, you've got a job for the summer," and that was that.

I'm going to be working for the Washington County Land Use Department and it's at the complete opposite end of the MAX line in H-------. Because my parents' schedules are so weird and I only just got my driver's permit, I'll be riding the MAX from one end of the line to the other end five days a week, back and forth, for the entire summer. I'm a little nervous about doing well at the job, but the Land Use people said that I'll do great. I'm mostly going to be doing research for them on that new measure that passed.

You've met my parents at parent-teacher conferences, but you probably don't know what they do for a living. My mom is a doctor, and she works some really random shifts in the ER. She's only been doing that for a year now, as she went back to school later in life and is just getting started in her career. My dad drives a big garbage truck for G---- Sa----- and he leaves every day at four in the morning.

I don't tell a lot of people that my dad is a garbage truck driver, but it's what he does. He loves it. In writing about my dad, I sort of wonder why I don't tell a lot of people about his career. Am I embarrassed?

I'll say this much—he's one very well-read garbage truck driver—he reads all the time. He earned his college degree in English.

We're not rich and we're not poor. My mom talks about med school loans from O--- a lot, but now that she's actually a doctor, I think she's less worried about them. My parents believe in hard work, and they most definitely believe that I can't just sit around during summer doing nothing.

I feel pretty good about the whole setup: I make some money at an easy job, I write these entries and read the book on the long MAX rides, and then I'll have time at night to hang out with my friends. Should be a pretty decent next couple of months.

By the way, did you notice where I wrote just a capital letter followed by hyphens? I'm sure you did, you're an English teacher. I just want to point those out so you know I'm doing the same thing Charlotte Brontë does in *Jane Eyre*. Sort of like when our middle school teachers made us underline our thesis or conclusion so they knew that we knew when we were doing them. I think Brontë does the hyphen stuff to conceal places and years or to keep her writing universal—could happen anywhere, anytime.

First day done, Ms. Warne.

Gresham Central Transit Center, Day 2

Ms. Warne,

I've pretty much grown up on the east side of Portland and lived here my whole life, but I've rarely had to ride the MAX. Recognizing my privilege here, I have parents who have been able to afford two cars and car insurance. Times were certainly lean when my mom was doing med school, but I've got nothing to complain about.

This one-and-a-half-hour ride both ways each day is going to be a whole new world for me.

It's only my second day into this whole summer routine, but I'm already making some observations. The first one is that most people on the MAX don't like to talk to other people. When I get on, I sit by myself—everybody does. We all look for a place where we can sit and not have anyone next to us.

Why is this?

Maybe we're all conscious of each other's personal space?

Maybe we all think each other smells bad?

Maybe we're all afraid or scared of each other—afraid we might actually get to know another human being?

It's sad, but the only time we "choose" to sit by someone is when we are forced to because the train is full. It's interesting to watch people's minds work out where to sit when they have to sit by someone, but still have a choice of who to sit by.

"Hmm, I can sit by the woman with the big purse or the old guy with hair growing out of his ears." I'll pick the purse lady. It reminds me of picking the right urinal to pee in at school when the other urinals are randomly in use. You do know that is a thing, right?

Now, I'm certainly not saying that we all should sit by one another on the MAX—I'm as guilty as the rest—it's just an observation.

The second observation I've already made is that nobody reads *Jane Eyre*. Nobody on the MAX is reading any of the "classics" that we read in high school. Sure, there are a ton of people reading, but they're all absorbed in what you like to call "popular fiction."

Just thought you'd be interested, Ms. Warne.

Gresham City Hall, Day 3

Ms. Warne,

I've always heard that you see and meet all sorts of fascinating people when you ride the MAX. I'm here to tell you that this is true. And it (seeing/meeting) happens even when we're all so busy trying not to talk to each other.

I'm sitting here trying to read and concentrate on *Jane Eyre* (what else?), and all of a sudden, I realize that the compartment I'm in has gotten quiet. And I mean even more quiet than it usually is—the kind of expectant quiet when you know something's about to happen and you're just waiting on edge for it to happen.

I'm sitting here sensing the quiet, and I look around and see that all of the other riders feel it too. They look like they're all thinking, "What's going on here?"

As if on cue, we stop at City Hall, and a single passenger gets on. He steps on and the hushed expectancy turns into a quiet murmur, almost reverie, amongst several of the other riders. I can't tell exactly what they're saying, but it sounds something like "the Prophet."

Before their hushed whispers register any meaning to me, the man begins to speak.

"Brothers and Sisters," he addresses us, "the time has come to talk of one thing."

He pauses.

"Life."

He looks us over.

"Yes, Sisters and Brothers. Life."

He pauses as if to give us time to think about that single word, "life." And then this guy does something that quite honestly scares me—he points directly at me and says, wagging his index finger all the while, "Life is not a destination. It is not something we arrive at."

Point at me, point, wag.

"You need to see life for what it is."

He looks at me eye to eye and says no more. The train stops, the doors open, and he gets off.

Just like that.

He was on the MAX with us for all of about one minute.

I look over at some of the other riders who don't look as shocked as I'm sure I do. One of the women in a fancy business outfit says to me, "You've never seen the Prophet before, have you?" I shake my head no, and she continues. "He'll come on board here and there and say some enigmatic things and then get off again. He's been doing it for years. People call him *the Prophet* because he gives advice and talks a lot about the future. Are you going to be riding the MAX often?"

I nod my head, this time in the affirmative.

"You'll probably see him again somewhere." And then almost as an afterthought, she says in a quieter tone, "Some people think he really can see into the future. He's said some things and known about things that even make me wonder if he's gifted that way."

Having said that, I think she is a little embarrassed because she quickly goes back to looking at her book.

Wow, Ms. Warne. It's only day three of me riding the MAX and things are already interesting.

Civic Drive, Day 4

Hey, Ms. Warne,

I decided that today I'd bring my laptop so I could write a bit more easily than just writing by hand what's been going on. That experience with the Prophet guy yesterday was pretty cool.

Civic Drive isn't a stop, Ms. Warne. It's just a sign right now, but I think they're going to make it a stop in the future. I'm including it as a chapter anyway.

So, I've got my computer out and I'm typing this as we go. I wonder what other riders would say if they knew what I was writing about. If they knew that I'm looking around writing—maybe writing about them? Would they care? Would they say, "Um, can you describe me this way?" or "I'm not really like that, am I?" Maybe if they knew what I was doing, they'd tell me to stop—that it's an invasion of their privacy.

Is it?

Maybe I shouldn't be sitting here watching people and writing and thinking about who they are and who they aren't and what they're doing and maybe even trying to think about what they're thinking about.

Kind of an interesting thought, isn't it? That all of these people I don't even know are now the subject of my thoughts—and even part of my life, sort of. The same lady who talked to me yesterday is on here again. We probably both have to ride the MAX at the same time to get to our jobs. I didn't see where she got off yesterday.

Over there is a business guy—he seems a bit preoccupied. There's a woman with her two little kids—probably taking them to daycare on her way to work is my guess. There's two, three, four, eight people toying with some paperwork because they think they need to be busy. Or maybe they really are busy.

There's—wait a minute. Is that someone I know? She looks like a girl at my school.

Janie? I'm pretty sure that's her name. Is that really her? Same dark hair, same intelligent look on her face. Plain but pretty cute. Yep, that's her.

I think last year was her first year at our school. What's she doing on here? I think she was in your class last year too, Ms. Warne—just a different period than mine. I did see her every now and then, but I never really got to talk to her. She must be smart if she's in your class.

She's typing on her laptop, just like me, and she keeps looking around and then typing some more.

Huh.

What if she's doing the same thing I am, writing about everyone else on the MAX?

What if she's writing about what I'm doing?

Kind of weird to think that someone else might be doing the same thing.

I wonder if she's reading *Jane Eyre*.

Ruby Junction/E 197th Avenue, Day 5

Dear Jane Eyre,

Ms. Warne—a letter to JE, so this is not for you. Read it, though, if you want to.

I'm in the early parts of reading your story, and I have a couple thoughts for you. Maybe even some questions.

I know you are a fictional character, and I know that Charlotte Brontë really wrote your story, but I'm addressing you since she set you up as the author of your own life.

In chapter 7, you write:

"My first quarter at Lowood seemed an age; and not the golden age either: it comprised an irksome struggle with difficulties in habituating myself to new rules and unwonted tasks. The fear of failure in these points harassed me worse than the physical hardships of my lot."

I must say you have captured almost perfectly how I feel about my first year at high school.

When I was a freshman, it seemed like I lost all of my friends. I grew up in a tight-knit neighborhood, and all the other kids my age were girls. I hung out with girls for pretty much all of my first eight years of school. My best friends were all girls.

But when we started high school, all of a sudden, I felt abandoned. It seemed like many of the girls that I had previously hung out with started to gain attention from older students (mostly boys), and I was left in the dust. As a ninth-grade boy, I often felt overlooked and unsure how to approach girls. What "rules," as you called them, had changed so suddenly? Did I miss a memo about societal changes once high school starts?

Of course, the upperclasswomen looked down on me as an immature, snotty-nosed delinquent who didn't have facial hair. I remember going to dances and looking around during the slow songs, not being able to dance with anyone. There was absolutely no way I could ask an upperclasswoman; they would brush me off or act annoyed. And all of the girls my age were already dancing with upperclassmen.

About halfway through the year, I thought I had a solution. My hypothesis was simple. To get back at these fickle girl friends of mine, all I would have to do is ignore them as we all got older. Come junior and senior year, those same girls who dropped me for older boyfriends would be clamoring for attention. They wouldn't want to socialize with puny, immature freshman boys; they'd want my friendship back, right? Brilliant hypothesis, yeah?

And then, when they came back to me, I would ignore them.

I would be flittering around, gifting my attention on the younger classes, just as preceding classes have done.

So, Jane Eyre, what do you think of my little idea? Brilliant? Well-thought-out?

What's that?

"How's that going for you?" you ask.

Well, I have to be honest, and now that I'm going to be a senior, I do admit I had some really stupid ideas when I was a ninth grader. I was a work in progress then, and I still am. I have certainly abandoned the dumb ideas of the past of ignoring people now that I'm older.

I don't know you super well yet, but you seem pretty smart and pretty resourceful. Would you have ditched me if I had been your friend and we went to a new school together? Would you still have been willing to be a girl friend of mine?

I am starting to enjoy reading your book now that I'm getting used to the fancy language. Don't tell my teacher—I gave her a bad time about requiring us to read it.

Sincerely,

Ty Clark

Rockwood/E 188th Avenue, Day 6

Ms. Warne,

Back to writing by hand again. The laptop was too bulky. Besides, I like writing in my notebook.

I'm not sure where my writing on the MAX today is going to take me because I've got a really random subject rolling around in my head: punctuation.

It all got started when I was just sitting here, mindlessly looking over the crowd on the train, and I saw another kid listening to music on his iPod. In my mind, I saw the name "iPod" and before I knew it, I was back in your classroom listening to you lecture our class about our inability to correctly use punctuation.

Ms. W: Punctuation hasn't always been around, nor is it the same today as it was when it first began way back when. In fact, it's my opinion that because of technology, specifically texting, punctuation and even capitalization will soon be seriously different than it is now. How many of you that have phones use them to text?

(Some hands go up. Mine does not, nor does the super smart girl whose parents choose not to own a TV.)

Ms. W: How many of you that text capitalize the letter *I* when you text?

(Only one hand goes up.)

Jill: (a bit pompous) I always capitalize when I text, Ms. Warne.

(Jill would. She's destined to be an English teacher—and consequently, she's a schmoozer in class. I think you already know she's a schmoozer, Ms. W. You're too smart to not recognize when students are sucking up to you.)

Ms. W: You texters have proven my point, I think. Already, most of you who have phones choose not to capitalize the letter *I* because it's inconvenient, yet you still get your meaning across. Does anyone know why we capitalize the letter *I* when it's by itself? Does anyone know when that started? Was it always capitalized?

(Nobody knows—Jill thinks she knows, but is wrong.)

Ms. W: Think of the names of punctuation marks. Period, comma, exclamation point, apostrophe, colon, semicolon—now there's an interesting name: semicolon. Have you ever thought about why we call these two marks of punctuation a colon and semicolon? Why did we name the semicolon and its twin after a body part that deals with waste disposal? Maybe that's why you students don't use a semicolon correctly very often!

(Low blow, Ms. Warne, low blow there.)

Ms. W: I can hear you when you're talking to the semicolon under your breath as you're writing your essays: "First of all, you're aligned with body waste. Second of all, you're not even a real colon—you're half a colon. There's no way I'm going to give you any respect, you dastardly piece of punctuation puke!"

(Of course, by now, all of us students were either laughing our heads off or in shock over your passion about punctuation.)

Ms. W: (bowing your head) Let us all give a moment of silence for the semicolon, please. Pillaged, then bludgeoned to death. Pity, since it was a case of mistaken identity. The intended target: the comma, of course.

Back to reality here on the MAX, I smile a bit, thinking about that day in class. You are a little weird, Ms. W., but we like you anyway.

And you know what? I looked up the history of the letter *I*. It wasn't always capitalized.

E 181st Avenue, Day 7

Ms. Warne,

Since TriMet came out with their get-tough policy about what happens if a person gets caught on the MAX without a ticket, I have been extremely paranoid about making sure I have my pass. I find myself checking my backpack three to four times during the ride to make sure it (the pass) is still there. It makes for a tougher time to concentrate on *Jane Eyre*, that's for sure.

Today, there was a ruckus because some lady got caught without her MAX ticket. And here's the ironic thing—this lady was rich. I don't know if she was just in a hurry or forgot or just felt like she was above the rules, but she flat out did not buy a ticket. Maybe she thought nobody would check—it is indeed very rare when they do.

I think I know this lady had money because of the facts that I observed: (a) she had on some expensive-looking clothes, shoes, and shades, and (b) she had a bunch of shopping bags from Pioneer Place mall. (My point is that she certainly could have afforded a MAX ticket.)

Two MAX officers got on either end of the car like they do, and I dug through my backpack to fish my pass out. I showed the officer my pass and then turned my attention to the rich lady because I could see the other officer standing in front of her, and she wasn't moving.

Pretty soon the other officer (the one who checked my ticket) was called over by the other worker so both of them were now talking with "Ms. Rich."

It didn't take long for her voice to be loud enough for me to hear what was going on from where I sat.

"What do you mean you're going to fine me 250 dollars? That's insane! The ticket is just $2.50 to ride the stupid thing. Here—" She threw a five-dollar bill at one of the MAX officers. "I've paid now."

"It doesn't work that way," one of the officers said to her.

"What do you mean it doesn't work that way," she shrilled. "I just paid you twice as much as the fare costs!"

The second officer remained extremely calm and said, "You tried to get away with riding the MAX without paying. You have been caught. You will either pay the fine or we can call the police."

The woman was really getting worked up now.

"I'm not going to pay anything, and all of you will have to talk with my lawyer. If you call the police, my lawyer will see to it that you all lose your jobs."

I guess, Ms. Warne, that this last statement of hers pushed some of the other MAX riders "over the edge" so to speak. Having witnessed all of this, and hearing this lady's elitist attitude, some of the riders decided to get in on the act.

"Hey, lady," one person said, "you got caught. You should've paid like the rest of us."

"Yeah," another chimed in. "What makes you think you're above the law?"

"Just because you have money doesn't mean that you can do whatever you want," said the woman who told me about the Prophet. Her name is Ruth by the way. She introduced herself to me a day or two ago.

I was really surprised by these outbursts because most riders usually pretend not to see anything going on around them.

Clearly this lady (and issue) struck a nerve somewhere, as more and more of the riders near her began reprimanding her for trying to get away with not paying for a ticket.

Sensing that the entire compartment was against her, she caved. "All right, give me the damn ticket." (She said more than damn, but I'm keeping this PG-13, Ms. Warne.)

When the officer ripped out the fine notice and handed it to the lady, a minor cheer erupted from the other passengers. Justice was served today on the MAX.

A little limerick to end today's writing, Ms. Warne:

"No Ticket"

There once was a rider with no ticket
Who thought she could lickity-split it
When the MAX people came
And they called out her name,
She told them right where they could stick it.

E 172nd Avenue, Day 8

"Hitherto I have recorded in detail the events of my insignificant existence . . . But this is not to be a regular autobiography: I am only bound to invoke memory where I know her responses will possess some degree of interest" (Chapter 10).

Ms. Warne,

Janie sighting number two. I'm starting to wonder if there is more to this than just coincidence. I'm kind of hoping there *is* more to this than just coincidence. As Jane Eyre remarked in chapter 10, this might be interesting.

I'm sitting here in my seat minding my own business, trying to read a little, when I look up and see Janie sitting across the aisle and over one seat from me. She's busy typing on her laptop again.

I watch her for a few minutes as she is intent on what she's doing.

Then, she looks up and I'm caught "red-handed" (whatever that means) staring at her. I'm a little embarrassed, so I quickly look down.

"You're reading *Jane Eyre*," she says.

"Unfortunately," I say, trying to sound more interesting than I really am.

"It's not that bad."

"You're reading it too?"

"Yeah. I'll have Ms. Warne again. She's weird, but I like her." Sound familiar, Ms. W?

"Your name's Janie, right?"

"Yes. You're Ty?" I nodded yes. "You started on the writing assignment yet?"

This is where things get a little tricky because I've got to say something that (a) is not too nerdy, (b) is not too non-nerdy—this girl is smart, after all—(c) shows that typical smart-kid, nonchalant-ness that implies laid-back teen attitude, and (d) is at least slightly impressive.

"I've started it but still have a lot to do." (Safe, but still suave, right?) "How about you?"

"Yeah. Me too. How far are you in *Jane Eyre*?"

"Page eighty-five. And you?"

"I'm done."

"You're done? Already?"

"Yeah. I got into it. It's a good story."

"Yeah, it's okay. It's getting better."

Awkward pause where both of us aren't sure what to say next.

Luckily, I think of something. "I saw you a couple weeks ago on the MAX."

"I volunteer at the zoo four days a week and ride the MAX there. You heard of the ZooTeens program?"

"Yeah. You like it?"

"Yeah. I like it a lot. I get to be with animals. I want to be a vet someday."

"That's cool."

Another bit of silence, and then I say, "What are you typing on your computer over there?"

Up to this point, Ms. Warne, I think I had been doing okay in the socially acceptable, conversationally correctness category, but clearly the question, "What are you typing on your computer over there?" was not the right thing to ask.

Janie's face turned a bit red, and she didn't seem to know how to reply, at first. She was quick enough to say, "Oh, nothing, really. Just some stuff for the zoo." But I had the feeling that this was not entirely true. Her embarrassment and her little pause (not to mention the fact that she slowly closed the laptop) made me wonder, more than a little, what she was doing.

I didn't want to cause any more weirdness between us, so I let it drop. But something made me think that maybe she was writing something she didn't want me to know about . . . or even, perhaps, see?

She got up to go—her stop, I guess.

"See you around," I said.

"I hope so," she said.

And before I could think much more about what that might mean, she was out the doors and gone. Kind of like that Prophet guy.

E 162nd Avenue, Day 9

Hey Ms. Warne,

I was sitting there minding my own business (as was everyone else) when a man stepped onto the train. It wasn't the Prophet, who I've kind of been watching for, it was just some guy. And he was smoking. Smoking weed.

Smoking Anything + the MAX = Against the Law

I know I was shocked to see such a blatant breaking of the rules, so I assume most of the other riders were shocked as well. We all just sat there, not moving, not saying anything.

The train filled with the skunky smell. "Why doesn't someone do something?" I thought. I looked harder at the No Smoking signs, as if my staring at them would help the man realize he wasn't supposed to be doing that.

The staring didn't work.

He kept on smoking.

For two stops, we all just sat there.

And then . . . he got off, all casual and slow and methodical as if nothing had happened. I peeked around to see the other riders' reactions—some looked indignant, some looked guilty, some relieved, and someone even murmured, "The nerve of that guy."

The MAX driver's voice abruptly came on the loudspeaker. How she ever knew that someone had been smoking, I'll never know. "Hey," the driver said a bit testily, "the next time anybody steps on the train and is smoking, you need to tell me *immediately*. All of you need to help me enforce the rules."

Wow.

I guess I'd never thought about it before, but the slightly peeved MAX driver was right. Us riders could have done something, but we just sat there, either too scared to do something or too timid to stand up for the rules. Were we afraid of the conflict? Afraid the guy might blow smoke in our faces? Did we think someone else would say or do something and so, in the end, none of us did anything?

The whole event has made me think a lot about right and wrong and responsibility. Because I spend a lot of time in classrooms, I'm mostly thinking about how this relates to our high school.

How many times have I turned my back to some offense at school and then perhaps even griped about it? If I'm truly disgusted by kids making out in the hallways, then why don't I tell the two offenders to knock it off? (I don't really care; I'm just using it as an example). If I see kids leaving their garbage in the commons after lunch, then why don't I tell them to pick it up?

The train driver's words have certainly caused me to wonder more about my role as a member of society.

Really, when I think about it, Ms. Warne, the only way you teachers have control of the classroom is because we students give it to you. If every single one of us students in AP English never stopped talking, then there's really nothing you and the administration could do about it, right? Sure, there might be outside pressures and consequences, but when it comes down to it, my freedom and rights are based on giving away some of those freedoms and rights and expecting everyone else to also give up the same things. In return we get civilization.

My head hurts.

Maybe it's from the marijuana smoke. Or maybe I'm just doing too much thinking during the summer.

E 148th Avenue, Day 10

To the meager class of 20--

(sorry, Ms. W, this one's not for you—it's kind of like a fun speech)

Over the weekend, I hung out with Omar and Jay, and we started talking about our upcoming senior year and reminiscing about our first three years of high school. We talked mostly about our freshman year, and while conversing about that year, we compared our class to the previous crops of freshmen who have graced the hallways of our high school. Our conclusion: the new breed of ninth graders have no respect for upperclassmen.

How has this injustice come about? The class of 20-- must share in some of the blame. As freshmen, our class took severe "beatings" (not really beatings, that's hyperbole—I know our being hazed or bullied is far less rough than the years of swirlies and penny pushing that my dad talks about) from the upperclassmen. They knocked books out of our hands; they grabbed our hair or flicked our ears when they sat behind us in classes we had together. Other demeaning activities were forced upon us. And hey, we respected the seniors when we were lowly ninth graders. That senior class even beat us that year in the Homecoming Float competition, something which no other senior class has been able to do. You do remember that our class has had the best float the past two years, right Ms. Warne?

But what about this upcoming year—our senior year? Will there be any initiation going on? Any hazing? Any bullying? No.

Will the ninth graders respect the senior class? No.

Will they be scared of us, as they ought to be? No.

When I was a freshman, I'd walk around the hall like I was a half-back weaving through the defensive onslaught. I'd be jumping here, dodging there, all in an effort to not bump into a senior. Will that occur when school starts back up in September? I doubt it. We're all too nice.

The freshmen will walk down the hall like they own the place. They won't move out of a senior's way. And what will the "nice" senior class do? We'll move out of their way! We ought to be ashamed of our inability to live up to the mighty senior name!

Have I made my point, fellow students? Have I enraged you to the point where you want some respect? Good. Go out and do something about it. We only have one more year, so we have a lot of work to do in a little time. Here's my plan and my call to action:

(a) We all need to begin giving freshmen the proverbial cold shoulder. We can't call it initiation or bullying—that's not right. We need them, though, to be scared of us.

(b) Books may need to end up on the floor . . . Too much? Figure something out that's safe but sends a message.

(c) Ignore the freshmen!

(d) Stand firm in the hallways, and make the freshmen get out of the way.

(e) And finally, take up the attitude that you are a senior, and that you own the school. Display your attitude to make the freshmen feel as insignificant as possible.

We are near-seniors and can't waste our rights and privileges that previous senior classes have had. Let's be sure to get with the program and teach this freshman class what they really are, just as we were taught when we were freshmen. Seniors, unite!

Just ignore this entire chapter, Ms. Warne. I re-read it, and it really is pretty stupid. You're probably saying to yourself, "Ty, what in the world are you thinking?"

I know. And I know better. And I know from experience.

I dreaded ninth-grade geography class because I knew the senior who sat behind me was going to flick my ear when the teacher wasn't looking. The kid had failed the class and had to retake it, and he found amusement in flicking my ear often. And it hurt. But I didn't say anything to anyone. I just took it for nine weeks until the teacher changed up the seating chart. I wish I had been treated better.

The school and world are better places when we treat each other with kindness and respect, no matter how I feel about my freshman year. Yeah, sometimes I want to be the tough senior. But mostly, as I've experienced in the last three years of high school, I've figured out that life really is better when we're trying to get through it working together, rather than trying to tear each other down. I really don't want other kids to have to put up with what I went through in that geography class.

Chalk a lot of my "here's where I'm at now" up to brain development and maturity.

So, yeah. I'd erase this whole thing, but I took a long time writing it, and I want to get credit for this project, so it'll stay. Hopefully you can see a little bit of introspection and growth in me, Ms. Warne.

E 122nd Avenue, Day 11

"A new chapter in a novel is something like a new scene in a play. . . . Reader, though I look comfortably accommodated, I am not very tranquil in my mind. I thought that when the coach stopped here there would be some one to meet me" (Chapter 11).

Hmm, Ms. Warne, hmmm.

As you can see, I'm about ninety pages into this roughly 460-page beast of *Jane Eyre*. It's okay, I'll give it that at least. It is a little eerie how that last passage is mirroring my own experiences today.

I had arranged to get off here at East 122nd Avenue to meet Omar. I think you know that he's my best friend. He would then get on the MAX with me and ride to my job where I'd worked it out with my boss to have him hang out and get a feel for what it's like in a Land Use office all day.

The problem is that Omar isn't here. Hence my connection with Ms. Eyre when I say that I too may look comfortable, but really, I'm a bit worried about my friend.

His parents are Iraqi, and they came here to the States after the first Gulf War. Life has not been easy for his parents, especially after various current and not-so-current events. The attack on the W----- T----- C----- has made things even harder on his parents and on him.

Omar is probably the smartest kid in the entire student body. You already know that.

And yet, here I sit at East 122nd Avenue, worried for him. Because he's not white he's always in danger. Always.

It's how it is here in white Oregon. Anytime Omar goes outside, he's in danger. And Omar knows that. And what is so amazing about Omar is that he isn't scared of other people. Whenever someone makes a stupid comment about Muslims or Islam or Iraq, Omar will let them know about it. Not in a mean, angry, jerk kind of way either. He'll call people out in a way that makes them want to listen to him instead of get mad at him.

He wasn't always like that, though. He used to be too scared to say anything. A lot of people don't know that Omar used to be this quiet kid that would rather play down his Middle Eastern background. He wanted to fit in.

It was in our freshman year that some teacher had a guest speaker come talk to our class. This guest speaker guy served in the Gulf War, and he came to talk to us about what it was like to serve in the army and be in a war. I didn't know Omar very well then—just knew he was quiet and not the same race as me. I didn't know his parents were from Iraq. And apparently, neither did the teacher? (Or they hadn't given it much thought.)

This guest speaker was in a tank brigade during the Gulf War and basically told us how easy it was to kill other tanks. "It was like playing a video game," he said. "I was in my tank, I'd see an enemy, I'd push a button, and boom! I'd just have blown up some Iraqi bad guy."

Most of the other kids were saying, "Cool" or "Awesome" or laughing at how easy it had been for the Americans to annihilate the Iraqis.

Not Omar.

And not me either. This guy's speech actually made me think more about war than I had ever previously thought about it before. His lack of regard (or disregard) of human life was pretty scary to me. His words kind of started to get me thinking more about why war is bad. I'd never really thought of war as a bad thing—I had always thought American involvement in war was positive. I got that from my dad, who is pretty upbeat about the United States. Ironic that this former soldier's glorification of US supremacy actually made me start to question national policy and attitudes.

Anyway, back to Omar. This soldier guy started to say a little more about Iraqis being "no match for our military might" when Omar stood up, said something I won't repeat to keep this assignment school appropriate, and then launched into a five-minute discourse about the negative historical and moral implications of the United States' imperialistic advances.

I don't think our teacher knew five of the words Omar used in his reprimand. It was for sure that I didn't know them. And I was very, very sure that the former soldier guy certainly didn't understand them.

Acknowledging my blatant stereotyping there of military intelligence, Ms. Warne.

The teacher was also shocked because this skinny little kinda-brown, kinda-olive kid who hadn't said two words all year was suddenly shouting obscenities and lecturing the class on US foreign policy.

I still remember part of Omar's conclusion: "How many of you can even pass the test that immigrants have to take to become US citizens, huh?" Omar then looked at the soldier guy.

"Soldier guy, can you name the three branches of government? How about who wrote the majority of the Constitution? How about naming three of the original thirteen states? No? I didn't think so. And you think you're an American?"

Wow.

Wow.

Wow.

Of course, Omar got into trouble, but not really that much. And ever since that day, he's been the Omar that I (and most of our school) know and respect. From quiet, timid Omar to outspoken, passionate Omar. After that day, I started hanging out with him because I liked how he stood his ground.

Back to the present, Ms. Warne. I'm still sitting here at East 122nd Avenue, waiting for him.

And here he comes—with two guys trailing closely behind him. One has a mullet and a shirt that says So Damn Insane. The other guy has a shaved head with more studs on his face, lips, and ears than a punk belt. It looks like all three of them are fired up.

I stand up and nod at Omar to hopefully let these guys know that I'm here to meet him. I can command a presence when I need to. Thanks to my mom and dad, I'm a pretty tall kid. I could feel my body start to tense up as I assumed the worst: that these guys were harassing him. All of them see my nod and walk closer to me as I brace myself for the possible confrontation. And while I'm worried about Omar mostly, I'm also worried for myself.

"Hey, Ty," says Omar. "I want you to meet Devin and Forrest. We've been talking economic policy together."

"Hey," they say to me.

"Hey," I say back.

"We don't agree with Omar on everything," the one with the studs says, "but we do all agree that the current American fiscal, fiduciary plan for foreign implementation isn't sound."

The next MAX pulls up, Omar says, "See you around" to his new pals, and we get on the train to go to H----- and my Land Use job.

"When I saw those two guys with you, I thought for sure they were giving you crap or worse," I say to Omar when we are sitting on the MAX.

"Not at all," Omar says. "I got to the MAX stop early and those guys were there, and we started talking."

"They weren't giving you grief? You all looked fired up," I say.

"When are you going to learn, Ty, to not be so judgmental? Just because people look a certain way or wear a certain shirt or even *believe* a certain thing doesn't mean you can't learn from talking with them. We were all very passionate about our opinions. What's wrong with that?"

I clearly still have a lot to learn, Ms. Warne.

E 102nd Avenue, Day 12

Hi Ms. Warne,

Gray. Grey. Greigh. Grae. Grai.

Whether or not we admit it—or even adamantly deny it—gray is our favorite color here in Oregon. It has to be. Why else would we live here? I wonder if it's our state color. It ought to be—trying not to use the word "should" anymore, as I'm learning from my parents that should is a shaming word.

If we had one "true" college team here in Oregon, the jersey colors ought to be gray and more shades of gray, not orange and black, or green and yellow, or purple and white.

I know there are so many different ways to describe gray. That one lady who wrote *Jump Off Creek* that you had us read last year, she said that Oregon skies were the color of an oyster. I liked that. But it's not the only gray.

I've decided (and yes, I'm writing about this because it's raining *again*) that we need to patent our gray—trademark it, copyright it, and then make some money off it. We'll call it "Oregon Gray" and anytime writers want to truly impress upon the reader the sense of the word gray they can use "Oregon Gray" to quickly help the reader know exactly how to feel.

Oregon Gray would equate to:

our famous "Oregon sunshine"

feelings of sadness and depression that come from one hundred days straight of rain

the boredom of not going outside for a month

the feeling of high school tennis matches being rained out day after day after day

the feeling of crying at anything anytime because we've been watching the sky cry for weeks

the resignation that it is raining today, but also a sort of hopeful expectation that tomorrow might be at least a lighter shade of gray

the beauty that gray brings: green

Maybe we can even have "Oregon Gray" and "Oregon Grey" and let authors use the alternate *a* and *e* to represent a subtle difference in tone or feeling.

Light grey. Dark gray. Ash. Charcoal. Black mixed with white. White blended with black. Oregon Gray. Oregon Grey.

Gray.

Gateway/NE 99th Transit Center, Day 13

Hey, Ms. Warne,

Still raining today, but it's supposed to be the end of it. I don't mind the rain for the most part. Kind of funny how in the summer when we don't get any for a while we Oregonians start missing it.

We were just about to pull into the Gateway stop when the rain really let loose. I sure was glad I was already inside the MAX and not trying to get on board like . . .

Janie.

As we were pulling in, I saw someone getting out of a car. That someone looked like Janie walking toward the MAX. Sure enough, upon closer inspection, it was her.

And she was getting soaked.

And she didn't care.

Most people would be running for cover trying not to get wet or, Portland forbid, have an umbrella with them.

Not Janie. It seemed like she was loving every second of the deluge. She was taking her own sweet time to get to the station and the MAX doors.

By the time she got her ticket and got on board, she was soaked. Other less sophisticated writers would say she looked like a wet dog, but she didn't. She actually looked . . . radiant? That's an interesting word for me to use here, Ms. Warne, but she really did look that way. I've never seen someone look like that coming out of a torrential downpour.

The MAX wasn't too full today, so I watched where she went and sat down and saw that there was an empty seat near her. I headed toward her, remembering her words, "I hope so," and found myself hoping that she meant those words.

As I got near her, she saw me.

"Hey," I said, and sat down next to her.

"Hi," she said, wiping water from her face.

"It's a little wet out there," I said.

"Yeah . . . just a little." She smiled. "I probably look like a wet dog."

I laughed. She ran her hand through her wet hair, which was even darker now that it was soaked through.

I wanted to say, "You look great," but I didn't have the guts. Instead, I said, "You don't look like a wet dog."

And then I remembered something. I opened my backpack. "My dad always makes me carry a handkerchief with me. Want to use it?" Kind of random, I know, Ms. Warne, but my dad really does make me carry one.

"Thanks. I'll take it." She wiped off her arms and her face a little.

"Were you getting dropped off by your parents?" I asked. She looked confused, so I continued, "I saw you get out of a car back there at Gateway."

She hesitated for a second or two. "Oh, no, that was a family friend."

"Cool—were you hanging out with them and they dropped you off?" Remember last time, Ms. Warne, when I asked her the question about what she was writing and that seemed to be the wrong question to ask? I had just asked another one of those kinds of questions, and I'm not sure why. It seemed like a pretty safe question, but again, Janie looked a bit embarrassed and seemed a bit unsure how to answer. The smile went away.

"Yeah—you could say that we were hanging out . . ."

It almost seemed like she was about to say more but then she stopped short.

And changed the subject.

"How's your internship going?"

"Good," I said. "Looking up land use records is just how I want to spend my summer." She smiled a bit at my sarcasm. "I like it fine," I said. "It is interesting. How goes the zoo?"

She smiled again and it was apparent that the zoo and the animals there brought her a lot of enjoyment. "It's amazing. There are these two otters, Trixie and Nixie, that I get to work with. They're adorable."

And the rest of the ride—until we neared the zoo stop—was Janie telling me all about Trixie and Nixie.

"Here's my stop," she said. She stood up as the doors began to open.

I got a bit bold.

"It was great to see you," I said.

And then she walked toward the now open doors but turned around just before exiting. "Thanks for letting me use the handkerchief. Since it's wet, I'll wash it and get it back to you the next time I see you." And off she went.

I had forgotten about the handkerchief.

NE 82nd Avenue, Day 14

Ms. W,

I was bored today on the ride over to H-----, so I started reading some of the stuff they put up on the walls of the MAX. You might not know this (Do you ever ride the MAX?) but sometimes they put up poems for people to read. Here's the one they put up on the wall where I sat today. It's by someone named Bev St. Anthony:

"My Boyfriend is My Socks"

My Boyfriend is My Socks
I slip my feet into his presence
force my toes into his 100% cotton
and wiggle his warmth around my little piggies.

Okay, Ms. Warne. What is this stuff? "My Boyfriend is My Socks?" "Wiggle his warmth around my little piggies?"

This is poetry?

It's no wonder nobody reads poetry anymore when all this contemporary stuff is so weird and well, so . . . well, weird. I don't get it at all.

And why doesn't TriMet put up any old-school poems like the ones we study in school? Where's Langston Hughes? Or Emily Dickinson? Or Gwendolyn Brooks? (Her "We Real Cool" poem is amazing.) At least we can understand their poems.

All I see right now are new poems that I can't understand.

Okay, I just wrote "can't" and that reminded me to re-story my story like we've learned about in Advisory class.

Growth mindset here.

Currently, Ms. Warne, I don't understand newfangled poetry. Perhaps you can teach us some modern poetry next year to assist me in understanding something other than the classics.

Help me, Obi-Warne. You're my only hope.

NE 60th Avenue, Day 15

"I believed in the existence of other and more vivid kinds of goodness, and what I believed in I wished to behold" (Chapter 12).

Ms. Warne,

I finally got a copy of *Jane Eyre* as an audiobook from the Multnomah County Library and I was intently listening and following along in chapter 12 when the Prophet walked onto the train again.

I took off my headphones so I could hear what he was going to say.

"Sisters and brothers," he began, "the time has come to talk of one thing. Existence. Yes, brothers and sisters, existence."

A pause.

"How do you," pointing at a person, point, point, "know you exist?" He didn't point at me like he did last time. "How do you know that anything outside of this moving structure exists? Do not trust your eyes, my sisters and brothers, because seeing is not proof of existence."

"Can you see love?" he continued. "Or hate? Or fear? Are those things not real?" The MAX was slowing down and I could see he was ready to get off. His parting words: "The unexamined to be is not worth being."

The MAX came to a complete stop, the doors opened, and he was gone.

What the heck, Ms. Warne? What the heck? What is this guy talking about? And why does he get on the MAX, say his little maxims, and then just disappear? Who is this guy?

I felt a little nudge on my shoulder. I turned to look and see who it was. It was a little old lady looking intently into my face. I'd ridden with her before. "What are you going to learn from the Prophet today?"

"What?" I asked.

She slowly reached for my hand and held it with both of hers. "What's your name?"

"Ty," I replied.

"I'm Betty. Nice to officially meet you. I'll ask you again, Ty. What are you going to learn from the Prophet today?"

"I don't know—" I started to stay, but Betty cut me off.

"That's your problem. You don't know." She didn't say it in a mean way, so I didn't take offense to it. "I've been listening to the Prophet for a lot of years. When I've actually thought about what he's trying to tell us, my life has been the better for it." She patted my hand again.

"Before you start writing in that notebook of yours again—you're not the only one who is watching other people—I want you to think about this question. When are you going to start knowing?"

Hollywood Transit Center/NE 42nd Ave, Day 16

Movies and mass transit, Ms. Warne.

That's what's on my mind today.

Over the weekend, my parents had me watch a movie with them that I guess was a big-time hit back in the day. It was called *Ghost*. It had some famous actors in it, but I'd never heard of them. Aside from the potter's wheel scene that made my parents squirm a little bit, I enjoyed the film.

I think I kind of liked it because of those scenes on the subway system. I think it was in New York, right? With my riding the MAX every day this summer for three plus hours, I am beginning to consider myself a mini-expert, a connoisseur of sorts when it comes to transportation, and those scenes of the ghosts in the New York subway system were pretty darn cool.

Which is why I'm now sitting here on the MAX wondering about the MAX and the movies "he" has been in. I'm not much of a movie buff, so I don't know if any movies have been made featuring the MAX in it. Pretty lame showing if I say so myself.

The MAX needs a movie—one with gun-slinging, ghost chasing, intensely loud action. But wait—that won't really ever work because our mass transit system just doesn't have "the look." Since 95 percent of our tracks are above ground, movie directors just can't get that same claustrophobic and cacophonic feel and sound that they're looking for in a subway or mass transit system.

Really, a movie set on the MAX would not be very interesting. Sort of like my little summer project I've got going on here, eh Ms. Warne? I admit that this little "book" of mine probably doesn't make for the world's most interesting read (certainly not a film), but at least it's real, Ms. Warne.

It's real.

All of this has happened.

And everybody that rides TriMet knows it's real because they've had the same experiences—or at least experiences that are comparable.

Every rider has a story to tell—some just get written down. Written sometimes even while riding on the MAX. What's been your super cool story while riding the MAX, Ms. W? Have you seen the Prophet?

Maybe met someone you'd like to get to know more? Maybe after you read this summer assignment of mine, you can tell me about your experiences on the MAX.

If this were ever to be made into a movie, I'd want to be played by someone like that guy from the film you showed us in class last year. Remember showing us *Finding Forrester*? Rob Brown is the actor's name.

Now, Ms. Warne, you might right now be saying, "Ty, he's Black, and you're not," but (a) I don't think that matters and (b) it's not entirely accurate that I'm not Black.

You've met my parents at conferences. My dad is as white as you can get—all of his ancestors were from England and Denmark. My mom, though, has a different story. Her great-great-grandma was Black and her great-great grandpa (if you can call him that) was white. White and an enslaver. I'll let you mull that over, that little bit of history that nobody likes to talk about.

A few white successive ancestors and all those Mendelian Punnett Squares later, you get me, Ty Clark, looking like I look.

Ever wonder if you really know your students, Ms. Warne? Have you ever really looked closely at me?

Back to Rob Brown.

Black or white, I would want someone as good an actor as him to play me in the film. And I think you said that the director of *Finding Forrester* is from Portland, right? So, Rob Brown plays me and Gus Van Sant directs the show. Done deal.

This story of mine won't ever be made into a film anyway.

Lloyd Center/NE 11th Avenue, Day 17

Okay, Ms. Warne,

I'm gonna trust you on this entry. You can never, ever, ever tell anybody about what happened to me today. This is like super embarrassing, and so it's got to stay here between you and me. If you don't think you can keep this a secret or if you think you can't respect me after reading this entry, then stop reading *now* and go to the next entry. I definitely thought about not writing about today, but (a) I promised myself I'd do this every day, and (b) I have learned something about myself, which goes with my summer assignment, so here goes.

Still reading? Last chance to stop.

The day started out regular enough, but turned into something that was anything but regular. I blame it all on the Honey Bunches of Oats that I ate before I rushed off to catch the MAX at 7:05 a.m.

Three stops later, I started feeling sick.

Another three stops, my guts were churning.

Three more stops and I knew I was in trouble. I needed a bathroom and I needed one immediately.

I looked around for the bathroom and looked . . . and looked . . . and looked. It then dawned on me—what probably every other person in the entire Portland metro area knows—there are no bathrooms on the MAX. I also realized that there weren't bathrooms at the MAX stops. Why had I not realized that before?

Before I could do anything, the train began moving again, and with the slight sway, I couldn't hold back anymore.

I pooped my pants.

I know that sounds ridiculous and gross and grade-schoolish, but how else do you want me to say it without using profanity? I guess I could use the past tense and say, "I shat myself," and maybe that doesn't sound so much like a swear word.

I don't know if you've ever experienced that, Ms. Warne (and I guess I don't really want to know if you have), but besides being humiliated and embarrassed, having a pile of something brown in your underwear isn't the most pleasing, tactile experience of one's lifetime.

I got off at the next stop and walked up the stairs to try and get away from the people who might have noticed the stains that I realized were spreading on my newly purchased khakis.

In walking quickly up the street, I realized that some poop was falling from my boxers and out the bottom of my pants. I could only imagine some random hunter-gatherer person getting off the MAX, seeing my "droppings" later that day, and wondering what strange animal had been in Portland.

Talk about embarrassing.

I used my phone (that thing I carry around with me but don't like) and called my mom and told her what happened and asked her if she could come and get me. I called my boss and told him I was sick. (I actually felt fine at that point, but how do you tell your boss that you couldn't come to work that day because you had pooped your pants?)

I mentioned to you earlier that I learned something about myself today.

Of course, the first most obvious thing I learned is not to eat Honey Bunches of Oats before getting on the MAX. The second is that I don't like the feel of feces in my shorts.

But now that I'm safe in my own room writing this out, I realize that if I can survive this humiliating day, I can probably be okay with anything life might throw my way. I can live through hard things. Everyone has crappy things happen to them and the sooner we all just realize that, the sooner we'd all treat each other better—not rub it in when someone's going through a rough patch or smells really bad in third period. Who knows, but maybe they are sitting in a pile of poop. Or maybe it's just metaphorical poop and it still really stinks.

I also have to say that I realize how lucky I am to have parents who help me out. One night about a year ago, I woke up feeling sick and threw up on my floor. I went and told my dad, and he got out of bed, went to my room, and cleaned it up. Two days later, I told my aunt about what happened, and ever the "tell it how it is" type of person she is, she said to me, "Why did your dad clean it up? Was your arm broken?"

Like then with the throw up and now with this, my parents are pretty impressive. And I'm lucky to have them. So many kids my age don't have supportive parents.

I'm still holding you to your word that you'll never say anything about this to anyone.

NE 7th Avenue, Day 18

Ms. Warne,

Have you ever noticed how the MAX sounds like the beat to some current, hip-hop dance song? You know the kind with the mindless lyrics that get all of us kids moving at those school dances you love to chaperone?

I noticed that the MAX brakes sounded like *bass bass bass* when I got off for a minute to grab an orange juice from one of the quickie marts. Maybe I noticed this because I had rap on my brain, as the guy next to me was listening to his music and I could feel the bass emanating from his ear buds. I had bought my orange juice, made good time, and got back to the stop just as the next train was pulling up. The sound of the train squealing or grating against the tracks as it braked sounded like the pounding bass from that one song in particular—it's that one song that even you know by now because it's been played for years at school dances. It's almost as old as I am (hyperbole, I know), but DJs still play it at our dances because that bass just begs us to get moving.

The actual lyrics started going through my mind, and as they did, I began thinking of my own version of the song—how about one dedicated to the MAX? I hurried back on the train, opened my notebook, and started to write.

(With apologies to the artist)

(Actually, with a lot of apologies to the artist)

(But feel free to rap along with it, Ms. W.)

"I Like the MAX"

I like the MAX 'cause I cannot drive
The other riders all alive
When a dude get on with an all-zone pass
And a backpack for his class, we all ride . . .

"I dare you to stand up and rap that right now."

What? That voice sounded familiar . . . and it was a voice that I wanted to hear more of . . . but was not a voice that I wanted to hear say something like that right now.

Apparently, I had been so engrossed in creating my parodic rap that I had failed to notice a dark-haired, intelligent, cute seventeen-year-old sitting next to me and reading my creation over my shoulder.

You guessed it. It was Janie.

She said, "I read your rap."

"I figured."

"It's fun. I dare you to get up right now and show me what you've got. Show everyone here what you've got."

Ms. Warne, I'm curious as to what you would have done in my situation. Here's a girl that I've been thinking a little bit about lately. She's pretty cool, and she dares me to rap to the riders on the MAX. If I don't rap, I'll look like a scared nerd who can't be spontaneous. (And one who parodies rap songs for amusement.) If I do take her up on the dare, I risk looking like an idiot in front of a lot of people. And in front of her.

I sat there for a minute.

"You really dare me to do this?" I asked.

"Yeah."

"You promise not to laugh at me?"

"I promise. No laughing."

Again, I sat there.

What eventually pushed me over the edge was the realization of two things: (a) I'd probably never see any of these riders again (Ruth, Betty and the other regulars were currently not on board), and (b) I could, well, you know, kind of impress this girl.

"Okay. I'll do it. On one condition." I had just come up with a smart idea.

"Okay. What's the condition?"

"I get to read what you were writing about the other day on your laptop."

Now it was Janie's turn to sit there. Her face turned a little red like last time, and she hesitated a second, but then she said, "Okay. It's a deal."

I stood up. I looked at Janie.

She smiled. "I'll be your sound." Then she started to beatbox.

Are you serious? Is this girl serious? Who is this girl?

The other riders looked around to see who is making the beatbox sounds, and before I could lose my nerve, I dove right in.

Two minutes later, when it was all over and Janie stopped beatboxing, I sat down and looked around. "That was fun," Janie laughed.

I have to admit that it was pretty fun. (I'll try to include the entire rap at the end of the assignment, Ms. Warne.)

Apparently, though, not everybody else on the train agreed with her. The old people were looking at me like they thought I was a weirdo. A guy that looked twenty said, "That rap sucked," under his breath. Two little kids clapped their hands and asked me if I could do it again. The majority of the people acted like nothing even happened. An older woman who almost looked like Betty but wasn't said, "Can you come perform that at my grandson's bar mitzvah?"

Janie was still smiling—she looked good when she smiled—and said, "You really did it. I didn't think you'd do it." She laughed. And for some reason it struck me that, while she smiled quite a bit, she maybe hadn't laughed a lot in her lifetime. That fleeting thought ran away as quick as it struck me, as I watched her run her hand through her hair, and her eyes brightened as she laughed some more.

I smiled back and said, "Yeah, we did it." And then, "So now I read what you wrote."

There was a shimmer of nervousness from her, but then, "You're right. But I don't have my computer with me. The next time we meet on the MAX and I have my computer, I'll let you read what I wrote."

I started to protest a little but thought better of it. I had just rapped on the MAX with a cool girl acting as my beatbox and I knew I ought to leave it all alone.

Let the moment be the moment and enjoy it.

But I couldn't help wondering when the next time we met might be.

Convention Center, Day 19

Hello, Ms. W,

While waiting at the Convention Center for people to get on the MAX, a car drove by and I happened to glance at its bumper sticker. It's one I've seen a million times, but I've never really given it much thought: Keep Portland Weird.

What exactly does that mean? Keep Portland weird? Where did that phrase come from? Why is it so popular? Breaking down the phrase, I deduced a few things:

(a) Portland is weird

(b) It wasn't always weird

(c) People want to keep it weird

(d) Some people must want to make it "not weird," hence the bumper sticker admonishing all who see it to "Keep Portland the way it is"

I guess that's my question here. How is Portland weird? Weird compared to what? Boise? Seattle? Bismarck? Wichita? How has PDX earned the distinction of being weird?

When did it become weird?

I wonder if it has something to do with its suburbs. Portland is stuck right in the middle of a clash of two different cultures: the West Side with its traffic-laden hipsters, and the East Side with its often-conservative clientele who'd rather eat fast food than at a fancy restaurant. Stuck then is Portland, torn in two, trying to exist smack dab in the middle of the east-west imbalance. Portland is like a heart supplying blood to two different ventricles, and so itself becomes this conglomerated mass of . . . well, weirdness? I totally recognize that I'm stereotyping the suburbians of Portland here, Ms. Warne. We live on the East Side, and my mom is very liberal, and my dad is pretty conservative, and she loves fast food and he prefers a sit-down, black-tie affair. But I really have no other explanation of how and why Portland became weird.

Here's my little list of why Portland is weird:

(a) People don't dress up to go to plays and concerts

(b) We like public transit (Go MAX!)

(c) We like protests—my mom told me about us being called "Little Beirut"

(d) I'm having a hard time coming up with anything else here, Ms. Warne.

I'm just not really buying into the whole myth of Portland being weird. I like the bumper sticker that I saw the other day: Keep Portland Wired. At least that one makes sense.

Definition of weird: (a) unearthly or mysterious—hmm, not really Portland. The only things mysterious about Portland are the underground tunnels and why people from California move here; (b) odd, fantastic, of strange or extraordinary character.

Odd, no. Extraordinary, yes, Ms. Warne. I love everything about Portland, City of Roses, Stumptown, Rip City, Bridge City, P-Town . . . give it to me!

(c) Archaic: having to do with fate or destiny.

Maybe.

Maybe that's the fit.

Portland will play a part in my destiny . . .

Maybe.

Rose Quarter Transit Center, Day 20

Hey Ms. Warne,

I wonder if this has ever happened before or if it could ever happen again. I'm not sure when the MAX first started service or the last time the Blazers were this close to reaching the NBA Finals, but today on the MAX was crazy.

Not only are the Blazers playing in a huge playoff game but the Timbers also have a home game today. Put these two sporting events together and you have the makings of a mad MAX day.

It started out cool enough, with nearly everyone on the MAX wearing Blazers hats, Rip City shirts, jerseys, headbands, sweatpants, Blazers underwear—you name it, it was on display. It seemed like everyone was "into" tonight's game.

And then, three dudes fully decked out in Timbers attire, including the famous green scarf and get this—three plaid kilts and toy axes—got onto the train. I didn't think much about them, other than I admired their fandom, until I thought about how these three guys dressed in green seemed very out of place in the sea of Blazers red and black.

It didn't take long for the comments to begin. They came from three other men dressed to the hilt in Trail Blazers clothing—I had never seen the "Blazers blazer" until today, which one of them had on. Now that was one stylish piece of clothing.

"Where are your bagpipes?" said the one with the Blazers blazer. Did I mention that these three Blazers fans had probably stopped at a bar before getting on the MAX?

"Why don't you cheer for a real team?"

"Why don't you cheer for a real sport?"

"Whatcha gonna do with those axes? Hurt someone?"

The three Timbers fans were cool with most of it . . . at first. But when the Blazers ringleader dropped the f-bomb so quiet that only the few of us right by them could hear what he said, I knew we were all in trouble.

Because I was in the immediate vicinity, I sustained what is often called "collateral damage." Errant punches made their way to several of us that were sitting or standing there.

It really wasn't a fair fight. The Timbers fans pummeled those three Blazers guys and the toy axes weren't even used.

I've often wondered why at school we tend to make a circle around the two kids who are throwing punches at each other. I used to think that we did it mostly so we could watch the action.

But I now wonder if it's also because somewhere down in our ancestral DNA, we don't want to let the fighters get out of the battle. We are trapping them in a circle, making it harder for them to leave. They have to fight in order to get out. Walking away from the violence is harder now that they know they would have to walk through other kids and the embarrassment and shame of others seeing them leave.

Kind of ridiculous that we do that when I really think about it.

I guess that last part had nothing to do with this fight on the MAX, Ms. Warne, but it was a connection I just randomly made to school.

I'll let your imagination fill in the details as to what a fight between six big men on one small MAX car would look like. Here, I'll even give you some storyboard prompts, and you can doodle in the margins what you think happened.

Storyboard 1—Draw a square and then use stick figures to portray the opening shot. Don't forget to include me somewhere in the frame.

Storyboard 2—What happens next in your version of the fracas? Draw the usual square and include me somewhere in your frame.

Storyboard 3—What is the final, end shot of your film version of this melee? Again, don't forget to draw your square and include me inside it somewhere. Am I the protagonist in your storyboard or just an ancillary character?

The MAX, of course, came to a sudden halt; security was everywhere, and the six fans probably didn't make it to their games on time. Did your final scene on the storyboard include these fans getting hauled off to jail?

The rest of us (some a bit battered and traumatized) tried to gain our composure and finish the ride in peace. As to whether or not the Blazers made it to the Finals . . .

You know that already, Ms. W.

Some year we won't have to reminisce only about 1977.

Old Town/Chinatown, Day 21

Ms. Warne,

Just because my mom is a doctor doesn't mean that I know a thing about taking care of sick people, nor does it mean that I know how to help when a woman is having a baby.

This was certainly a ride I'll never forget.

All along the ride, we had been stopping every now and then for the usual mini-delays, and then while we were in the tunnel, we came to a permanent stop. The driver on the intercom told us that she apologized for the delay, but something was wrong up ahead and we were going to be stuck for a while. There were a few moans and groans from passengers, but one groan continued after the others left off. It was from the pregnant lady who usually gets off at the next-to-last stop, the stop before mine.

This lady did not look good. Some of the other passengers saw her too, and since some of them obviously knew what was going on (more than I did) they started walking over to where she sat. I heard the word "labor" and "going to have her baby."

What? Here on the train? How can a woman get on a train to go to work when she's in labor? Those were my first thoughts, but then I remembered the story my mom always told me about my birth. Since I was her first kid, she didn't really know what to expect from labor. She barely made it to the hospital, her water breaking in the elevator, and I was born ten minutes later with an overeager intern getting her first-ever delivery.

"Hey, Ty." My attention was brought back to the present situation by Ruth.

"Hey, Ty," said Betty, who was also helping the pregnant lady. "Come over here and help us."

"Me?"

"Yes, you. Come over here. This woman is in labor. We need to help her." That came from a man who I had seen before but not ever talked to.

I walked over to where the lady sat groaning and crying and moaning. Astutely, I noticed that her seat and the floor underneath her were wet.

"Uh . . . I think her water broke," I ventured. Another cry from the woman. Recollecting all the movies I'd ever seen about early deliveries, I said, "Maybe we ought to boil some water?" The looks I got after I said that were enough to tell me how stupid my comment was.

"My water did break," the lady managed to say. "I'm not due for another three weeks, but I think this baby is coming *now*."

In talking to my mom later that night, I learned that we should have just had the woman squat right there in the aisle and let gravity help that new little baby "fall out." But we didn't know that. Instead, we had her lay down in the aisle, and together the four of us little riders helped deliver a baby. I was the designated hand holder, who was instructed to just hold the woman's hand and tell her she was doing great. I got another of my dad's handkerchiefs out of my backpack and gave it to her to wipe the sweat off her face. She appreciated that.

Of course, we had called the driver via the emergency call button and paramedics had arrived soon thereafter, but not before a seventeen-year-old (me), Ruth, Betty, and two other guys helped deliver a baby girl in a tunnel on the train.

I made sure to check the *Oregonian* the next day, and sure enough, the story was there. I also found out the parents had decided on a fitting name for their new kid.

Maxine.

Skidmore Fountain, Day 22

Hi, Ms. W,

I hung out with Omar a little bit last night and told him about helping the woman give birth to her baby. Omar responded with a joke—he can be pretty funny sometimes.

Omar: Why did the man take his pregnant wife to the grocery store?

Me: I don't know. Why?

Omar: The man heard they had free delivery.

Writing that out, it's not that funny, but hearing Omar say it and watch him burst out laughing afterwards, I will say that it was kind of funny. Maybe you just had to be there.

Two words for you today: Voodoo Doughnuts.

I guess I don't know where you live, but since you teach on the East Side, I assume you live on the East Side, so you're probably like me and only get to drool whenever you hear those two words together.

Well, I had to have one of those cool, shiny pink boxes all to myself today, so I got off the MAX and proceeded to walk the short distance to the doughnut shop.

I could see there was a line—when isn't there a line?—but I didn't see who was at the end of the queue until I nearly ran into her.

Janie.

I haven't seen her since we pulled the rap stunt a while back. I will admit, I have been thinking about her since then. Smart, dark hair, fun personality, but not overly hyper. What's the word I'm looking for?

Depth. That's it, Ms. Warne. Janie's got depth to her.

And now here I am behind her in line at Voodoo Doughnuts. What are the chances?

She saw me as I was approaching the line, and I couldn't quite tell if the smile on her face meant she was glad to see me or just surprised to see me.

"Hey," I said. "Getting some doughnuts, huh?"

"Yeah. I'm taking them to share with everyone at the zoo."

"That's nice of you."

"I told them all about your rap. They all want you to come and perform it as the preshow for one of the Summer Concert performances."

"Ha ha, very funny," I said, although I was a bit pleased with her compliment. I was also glad to hear she had been talking to other people about me. That's a good sign, right?

"Speaking of my rap," I said, "You owe me now. I get to look at what you were writing that one day when I caught you looking around and typing."

"Oh yeah, that . . ." she trailed off.

By then, we were both in Voodoo, so we ordered and got our shiny pink boxes filled with glorious goodness.

When we got outside, I asked her again, trying not to come across as a jerk who was obsessing over what she had written. "So, you got your laptop? You can show me when we get back on the MAX."

We had started walking back to the MAX station, but she suddenly stopped, turned toward me, looked at me straight in the eye, and said very calmly and very seriously:

"Ty, if we meet twice more on the MAX this summer, I'll let you look at what I wrote. I just don't think I can share it with you yet." The serious look on her face and the fact that she had used my name told me not to argue the point by reminding her that our deal had been if I rapped, I could read. So, I let it go. Mostly, I let it go.

"How do I know you won't erase or change what you wrote?"

Again directly, and again using my name, she said: "Ty, I promise you that I won't change anything I wrote that day. Do you trust me?"

That caught me off guard.

I've seen so many movies and read a lot of books where that line is used that it has almost become one of your dreaded clichés, Ms. Warne.

But hearing Janie ask me that, I knew it wasn't a cliché. I could tell that she was putting a lot on the line by asking me that question. Whatever she had written on the laptop that day was a big deal, and she wasn't going to share it with just anybody.

"I trust you," I said.

She smiled. "Thanks. That means a lot to me."

We got on the MAX together, chatted about the zoo for a while, and then we were off on our separate ways.

And that was that, Ms. Warne.

I now need to run into her twice more this summer on the MAX so I can read what she wrote. It's gone from one time to two. And I'm okay with that.

Twenty days of work left, one month until school starts, and two chance encounters to try and finagle. I got this.

Oak Street/SW 1st Avenue, Day 23

Ms. Warne,

I am fully aware that some of my entries appear on the surface to have nothing to do with the MAX, the stop, or station under which said entry may fall. However, with careful literary analysis and/or explication (and a little imagination), it is clearly very easy to see how everything ties together. Just like how everything literary has some deep meaning, right? If "The Red Wheelbarrow" can elicit two days of heated debate in our class, then certainly you can figure out my little magnum opus.

So, while this entry has little to do with a MAX stop itself, it has everything to do with what I kind of feel that the MAX symbolizes.

My mom is a big-time jazz fan. Not the lousy Utah basketball team, but the real jazz—jazz music.

She and my dad both grew up here in Portland, so she knows the jazz scene, as she calls it. I guess there used to be this big time Jazz Festival in G-----, the Mount Hood Jazz Festival, I think it was called, and my mom and dad used to go to it all the time.

My mom still laments that this festival isn't around anymore, so the other night when she got wind of this jazz event thing in G----- on Saturday, she was pretty excited. My dad already had something else going on, so my mom asked if I wanted to go with her.

"Where?" I asked.

"Downtown G-----. There's going to be some good music." I probably looked a little skeptical because my mom's music and my music are not always the same. "I'll take you out to dinner if you come with me," she added.

"Okay." Few seventeen-year-old boys would be stupid enough to pass up dinner, right?

Here's the event, Ms. Warne: the City of G----- (or somebody, I guess) wanted to celebrate the fact that jazz is still around, and even though the big-time jazz festival doesn't happen anymore, there's still "all that jazz" floating around Portland. So, on Saturday, they had some live jazz at a bunch of restaurants and shops. The gig my mom really wanted to go to was a place called J----- B-----.

We walked in and sat down on two chairs in the corner of the place.

I'd never been here before, so I was checking out the decor, especially the big mural-like paintings of jazz musicians on the walls.

They had a piano set up in the middle of the establishment, and there was this older guy playing and even singing. I guess he sang most of the time, but I wasn't paying much attention to him. He had two first names—Tom Grant, I think. Another guy named Chris Botti was also there playing trumpet. I found out later that I actually share a birthday with the Botti guy.

Anyway, I was not so much listening as I was watching. There were a lot of people crammed into the store to listen to this jazz. A lot of them were old-timers, and as the evening progressed, they got this look on their faces as though they were somewhere else. Some faraway place, or time even, as I later talked to my mom about it. A lot of the older people knew each other, and they waved and whispered to each other throughout the evening—most of them talked to the owner of the café as well. I even saw Betty there and I introduced her to my mom. She bragged about me and how I helped deliver the baby on the MAX.

I don't know if it was the music or the people or the setting, but I got the sense of something this weekend, Ms. Warne. This is a thing that me and my generation have lost or have never had or have never experienced or never learned. And I don't know why we haven't learned it—maybe it's because of technology or the pressures we feel—I just don't know.

What I sensed and felt and saw Saturday night was a collective, shared sense of community—of getting together with people who share that same something with each other, even if for only an hour or two. Sure, the little grandma who sat in the corner lost in her memories may not have had anything in common with me, a seventeen-year-old kid, but that night, the love of jazz (or at least my mom's love of jazz) brought everyone together in a shared experience—a positive shared experience too, not some natural disaster or tragedy that brings people together out of desperation or survival.

I liked that feeling. And I want to feel it more often.

Bringing this all back to where I started. The MAX (or just MAX) offers the same communal experience for those who choose to embrace it. I ride with others who ride with me. Sure, all us Portlanders love the MAX because it's "green" and shows how we value the environment, but maybe there's more to the MAX than that.

Every day, every ride, the MAX becomes a community, a gathering place so to speak. Yeah, everyone does their own thing once on the train, but the possibility of shared experience and community is always there. It's always there just waiting for us to engage in it.

I left J----- B----- that Saturday night feeling a little older, a little more mature, a little more connected. And yes, my mom did take me to dinner.

But even if she hadn't, it would still have been worth it.

Morrison/SW 3rd Avenue, Day 24

Hey Ms. Warne,

A downer day on the MAX today. We had to sit and wait, not going anywhere because there was an accident.

Everything was going fine on my ride for the day when suddenly the train braked very hard. It wasn't like the movies when everybody is jerked around and riders crash to the floor—we just braked *real* hard, real fast and we weren't near a stop either.

Then, the waiting began. There was no word from the driver, no nothing at first. Then sirens, then fire trucks, then ambulances, and then police. Then, an announcement that there had been an accident and we couldn't go anywhere for a while, and they appreciated our patience.

Accident.

Accident.

Accident.

This word has haunted me for the past seven years. And I guess now is just as good a time as any to share something with you, Ms. Warne. And it's hard to write about. This might be hard for you to read too, Ms. Warne, so hopefully it will be okay.

I remember you telling us one time about Charles Dickens saying something to the effect of no matter how well you know somebody, that somebody always has something they don't share with you. No matter how well we know a person, we never know everything about them. Maybe that was in *A Tale of Two Cities*; I can't remember.

My unshared thing involves a brother that you'll never have as a student. When I told you at the beginning of junior year that I was the only kid in my family, it was not really true. I've never shared what happened to him with anyone, really, but I suppose if I can write and tell you that I pooped my pants on the MAX, I figure I can trust you with the death of my brother.

Seven years ago, my family was sitting in our house talking about taking a short vacation right before school would begin. I was ten and my little brother, Dom (short for Dominick), was seven. "Where might we want to go?" my parents asked us.

Looking back on this now, I can see the irony (sadly) in that it was Dom's idea to go to the water park. He had heard his friends talk about it, and he really wanted to go. My parents thought it was a great idea. So, to the water park we would go.

The day came for our mini family vacation, and we first went and saw a movie. (I can't even remember what we saw.) Then we went to lunch. My parents let us order anything we wanted off the menu, and Dom and I both stuffed ourselves on burgers and fries.

When we got to the water park, Dom could scarcely contain his excitement at finally being there. We quickly got dressed and went out into the very crowded water park. (Very crowded because it was such a nice day, and as you know, nice days in Oregon are hard to come by.)

This is where things become a bit blurry, Ms. W., so I'll do my best.

Somehow, we lost my brother.

Lost

track

of

him.

When I say "we," I mean me and my parents. I was ten, and I don't know if the crowds overwhelmed me or what, but I just remember my parents coming up to me pretty frantic, asking if I knew where Dom was.

And then we heard the whistle.

Everybody knows that lifeguards blow whistles to get someone's attention.

When I heard the whistle, I had that feeling that people get when something is wrong, and they know life as they previously knew it is about to change.

I looked over to where the lifeguard was standing. She blew her whistle again and then dove into the deep end of the pool. Seconds later, she surfaced.

Please don't be Dom. Please don't be Dom. Please don't be Dom.

When I saw the blue swim shorts, I knew it was Dom.

The rest of the experience is still surreal. Snatches of my ten-year-old memory still linger:

my dad rushing me into the locker room to get dressed

kneeling down by the car alone, praying to God that my brother would be okay

having a family meeting two days later where my parents told me they were going to take Dom off the life support system

the funeral where I couldn't stop crying

the nightmare I had all night long the day before I started fourth grade. It was a mere three days after the funeral. In this nightmare, someone kept breaking into our house and shoving me into the washing machine where I was drowning.

These memories are still very much a part of me, Ms. Warne, and have probably been a part of what has shaped me into who I am today.

My parents and I haven't really ever talked much about it. I can't imagine the sorrow, the guilt, the blame that they feel, because I know I feel it a little bit myself. But not as much as they do, I'm sure. Even now, I wonder about how that lifeguard feels—and now I wonder about the MAX driver.

My family has never really been able to figure out what happened that day, either. The newspapers, I guess, quoted a girl saying she saw Dom jumping off the diving board in the deep end, but we had a hard time believing that because Dom didn't really know how to swim. Why would he do that? How did it happen?

I was young—ten—so I did eventually heal, mostly move on, and even forget sometimes what happened that day. But, I suppose, Ms. W., that as I'm writing this on the MAX, I've realized that even if I couldn't figure it out then, I've figured out something now.

I lost a little part of myself that day. A part that I can't get back, at least not for a long time.

I've still never learned how to swim.

Yamhill District, Day 25

Hey Ms. Warne,

First a note about the chapter title. If you're one of those readers who check up on every little detail about whether or not the author knows what they're doing, then right now you'd be saying, "Ah ha! Caught you, Ty! The Yamhill stop only runs east, so you're out of order!" I will admit that I sometimes do that as a reader myself, and I will assume that since you're an English teacher, you do too.

You are correct, if you did indeed catch me, that the Morrison, Pioneer Square North, and Galleria/SW 10th stops only exist if you're heading west. The Library, Pioneer Square South, and Yamhill stops only happen when you're heading east.

Here's the deal, Ms. Warne. Sometimes I'm writing when I'm on my way to work and sometimes I'm writing when I'm heading home at the end of the day. So, while these six entries/chapters might seem out of order, then they probably are. I don't have enough days in the summer to write an entry for every stop both coming and going, so I'm jumbling these six all together. I hope you won't grade me down for the inconsistencies.

Today, I was sitting on the MAX on the long rows—a lot of empty chairs for some reason—when these two guys in white shirts and ties got on and sat down by me. They both had on a black name tag, so I knew who they were: Mormon missionaries.

One of my other best friends at school is a Mormon, so I know a lot about their church and beliefs. I know enough to clarify that the real name of their church isn't Mormon. But the real name is so long, it's easier to just say Mormon. They're good people for sure. It's odd now that I think about my religion and my best friends' religions. I'm Methodist, Jay is a Mormon, and Omar is a Muslim. I wonder if there's something sacred about the letter *M*? Maybe that's why all of those religions start with that letter?

Anyway, these two guys said, "Hi" and I said something like, "How's it going?" and they said, "Fine" and that was that. They got busy talking to themselves and I pretended to read *Jane Eyre*.

But having these two religious dudes next to me got me thinking.

My parents took me and Dom to church pretty much every week when we were little. Since Dom died, we still go, but maybe not every week now. Growing up with a fairly religious background, I have been brought up with the notion and belief that God sees all, knows all, and can do all.

I like the notion of God and I like the idea of an afterlife, especially because of Dom's death. I also like that there's someone always watching out for me and always cheering me on.

I'm not too keen on the heaven and hell thing, but I tend to focus mostly on the heaven part, and that helps me stay positive. I do think about religion quite a bit, especially since I have friends that have different religious beliefs. The cool part to me is that even though we have different ideas about religion, we all think there is a higher power out there, no matter what that higher power might look like.

Thinking more about God and God's job, I sit here on the MAX and my sometimes-overactive imagination kicks in: What if God quit his job and went on vacation to some far-away galaxy?

Would He still hear me pray?

Would water still run clear through a brook?

Who would take His place?

Would God take His American Express card with Him? Don't leave home without it!

Would He only take His wife for a romantic getaway or would His family go with Him?

Would the Earth decay and rot?

In pondering these questions, Ms. Warne, I never came up with any good answers.

Only more questions.

Mall/SW 4th Avenue, Day 26

From chapter 26 of Jane Eyre, Ms. Warne:

"Mr. Rochester was not to me what he had been; for he was not what I had thought him. I would not ascribe vice to him; I would not say he had betrayed me: but the attribute of stainless truth was gone from his idea; and from his presence I must go: that I perceived well."

Well, well, well, a little plot twist in *Jane Eyre*, eh Ms. Warne? Very clever of sly Charlotte Brontë to have the mystery woman be Rochester's wife. I didn't see that coming.

What will Jane do? Will she leave him "ere" the next day begins? Pun intended of course. Or will she err (ha ha!) on the side of love and stay with the wanna-be polyamorist? Or is it polygamist? In either case, it will have to wait, and I'll find out tomorrow, as I've got my own mini-drama to work through.

Janie.

I know it seems totally contrived that here I am reading *Jane Eyre* and this girl named Janie has entered (and possibly exited) my life just like Rochester in the book, but (a) that's her actual name, and (b) you assigned us the book, which I won't call stupid anymore, as I can see that it's clever. This Dickensian deus ex machina in my life coinciding with what I'm reading in the book is not my fault.

I'll spare you the details, but the short of it is that I saw her on the MAX today, but it certainly didn't go how I thought it would go. It was crowded and I glimpsed her on the opposite end of the compartment. I started to make my way through the crowd to talk to her so I could count it as one of the two meetings, but then I saw that some guy had his arm around her. To make matters worse, he had a J------ High School shirt on. It's the school that everybody loves to hate because they're so good at everything.

Anyway, I saw her. And then she saw me.

At least I think she saw me. Did she see me? Maybe she didn't see me. I don't know.

It was so crowded, I couldn't get any further through the people, so I just turned around and inched back to where I came from. I'm kind of upset and kind of mad, and yes, even a little hurt and jealous, Ms. Warne, because I thought Janie and I might have a little something started.

Mall/SW 5th Avenue, Day 27

Hi Ms. Warne,

It is hot today, way too hot. Portland only has one or two weeks a year when it gets too hot, and this is one of those weeks.

The MAX is running slower than usual, and the driver explained why. I guess any time it's over ninety degrees Fahrenheit there's something about electricity or connections or whatever that causes the MAX to have to slow down. Darn this ninety-degree heat.

Not only is MAX slow today, but it is crowded. I usually get a seat, but didn't today, so I'm standing.

The other thing this heat causes is smell. *S-M-E-L-L.* Most of the time MAX has its usual neutral-ish smell, but when it's ninety degrees and people are getting on and off the MAX, the smell changes. Drastically.

Today's smell is a combination of "flavors." First off is cigarette smoke from rider number one who gets on and presses in next to the rest of us who are already standing. Then at the next stop, two new smells are introduced: perfume and BO. The perfume is from a girl who looks like a ninth grader (it is only ninth graders who wear perfume) and the BO emanates from a big dude with a hard hat on his massive head.

These last two riders cram themselves in and before I know it, I'm surrounded.

Since we're all standing and holding on to the bar (get the drift [or whiff], Ms. Warne, all arms raised), I'm intaking a combo of three odors that do not play well together.

It's a good thing I didn't eat lunch today or I would have been like the guy next to me. Apparently, BO + cig + perfume = vomit for some people.

Chunks, Ms. Warne, chunks of . . . something came spewing out. At least I avoided it, unlike two others by me.

Not a pleasant ride today. Curse this ninety-degree heat.

Pioneer Square South, Day 28

A few numbers, Ms. Warne,

The number of TriMet boarders each year: 99.3 million

The percent of regular riders who say they like the job the MAX does: 77 percent

The number of crimes reported at the Mt. Hood Avenue MAX stop: 0

The number of crimes reported at the Gateway stop, the stop with the most crime: 66

The number of poems I've read here on the MAX: 22

The number of drug deals I've seen on the MAX: 2

The number of times I've seen someone offer up a seat to someone else: 10

The number of people on the MAX I've talked to that I didn't know: 7 (I've actually kind of got to know Ruth, Betty, and now Jeff, who ride regularly with me each morning)

The cost of a gallon of gas: $2.20

The cost of three gallons of gas to get me to and from work if I drove: $6.60

The number of words in *Jane Eyre*: 183,858

The number of people named Janie that I can't stop thinking about: 1

Pioneer Square North, Day 29

Ms. Warne,

Finally, a poem that was worth putting up on the MAX! This one was next to an ad telling me to "Strive."

"Memory"

How many times in a group
Have I felt alone?
I'm included,
Yet separate.

How many times all alone
Have I felt accepted?
I'm secluded
Yet befriended.

Memory fills the void that
sometimes strikes my soul—

A quiet chat, an evening stroll,
An extra-innings baseball game,
A ride on a bike.

All soothe my heart
And carry me to grandeur heights.

Memory: I guard it well, for
Once lost, I am lost.

How about it, Ms. Warne? Better than that "girlfriend is my toes" thing, yeah?

Clearly, the poet here does a masterful job of showing just how powerful and important memories are to the reader. Brilliant!

You were probably trying to recall all of your years of studying poetry in college to figure out and remember who wrote that poetic piece of perfection. I didn't write the name of the poet on purpose. Did you recognize who wrote it? Whitman? Plath? Gwendolyn Brooks? Adrienne Rich?

Ha! None of the above. It's me, Ms. Warne. I wrote that poem, and while it's probably not very good, and while it's probably not "real poetry" (whatever that is), I think it sort of proves my little hypothesis about poetry or any art that becomes famous or successful or important. The randomness of it all is mind-blowing.

What makes something a "classic"?

Why did anyone ever watch *Napoleon Dynamite*?

Why do billions of people line up at the Louvre to see *Mona Lisa*? Why do we still listen to the Rolling Stones? Why still read *Jane Eyre*? Why isn't my poem hanging up on the MAX trains, but Bev St. Anthony's poem is?

I guess I'd like to think that my poetry and my voice are just as important and just as valid as anyone else's. And their voices are just as important and just as valid as mine. What do you think, Ms. Warne? I've got a little room left on this page, so you can leave me some comments, either about my poem or about the nature of poetry in general. Is my poem destined for classic status?

Library/SW 9th Avenue, Day 30

List, Ms. Warne,

List, O List! If ever thy student thou didst love, check out this list of what people were reading today on the MAX. I know what they were reading because I walked around all ride long checking out the titles. When I finished one car, I'd get off at a stop and then get on again real fast on a different car. My long ride yielded the following:

Kindred (I think this was written by the same woman who wrote that super cool short story "Blood Child" that you had us read last year.)

The Lovely Bones

The Oregonian (the newspaper—several people were reading this)

The Bible

Blood Meridian

The Unbearable Lightness of Being

It

Harry Potter

The Oregon Driver Manual

The Book of Mormon

Classical Physics (a textbook)

Beloved

True Believer

Jewels (Danielle Steel)

The Pillars of the Earth (Ken Follett)

The Bachelor's Bargain (Harlequin romance—barf!)

Jane Eyre

Just kidding about *Jane Eyre*. Nobody reads that book but AP Lit kids.

Infinite Jest (That's a huge looking book—I wonder if it's any good. The title is cool.)

The Book of Laughter and Forgetting

Speaking of titles of books, Ms. Warne, I'm wondering about what I'm going to title this little summer assignment of mine. You're always telling us to come up with a title that's clever and engaging.

Let's see . . .

Letters to Ms. Warne? My Summer of Transit? Long Day's Journey on the Train? MAXed Out?

This is actually pretty fun trying to come up with something.

How about *Writing on MAX*?

None of those seem quite right.

I'll come up with something, Ms. Warne. I suppose you'll already have seen what I ended up calling it, since it will be the first thing you read when I turn this thing in to you. But you'll know that I actually put thought into what I end up calling it all.

Powell's Bookstore, Still Day 30

Ms. Warne,

There is no MAX stop at Powell's Bookstore.

But how, how, how could I not include Powell's somewhere in this summer assignment of mine?

So, I'm just going to include it here for fun.

For fun and to acknowledge that Portland would not be Portland without this place of all places, this store of all stores, this reader's paradise of all readers' paradises, this place that transcends time and space and everything else that can be transcended.

Clearly, I love to read.

And clearly, so do you, Ms. Warne. But I want to let you in on a little secret about my reading, and I know it's different, and I know it's maybe odd, but it works for me.

I will only read one book per author.

GASP!

Yes, I've said it out loud. One Brontë, one Rowling, one Morrison, one Walker. One.

Why?

Two reasons, and this kind of got started my ninth-grade year. A lot really happened that year, didn't it?

(a) I read *E---- G---* and loved it. Scooped up a few more books by the author and hated them. It took away from my liking of the first book I had read by that author and made me really question whether or not authors have more than one good book in them.

(b) There are millions of authors out there. If I'm going to learn from all of them, I can't confine myself to reading a bunch of books by just one and potentially miss out on others. My time on Earth is not infinite, and I need to read and learn from as many different people as possible.

So, before I read the book by that author, I do research and pick the one that is their best book.

"What if it's their first book and you want to read it?" you ask me.

If I choose to read an author's first book, then I'm taking the gamble that it's going to be their best book. Otherwise, I'll wait and see.

I have broken my rule once or twice since my ninth-grade year, and I'll probably have to break it again when teachers pick books I have to read. But on the whole, this little rule of reading has served me well.

Maybe you'll want to consider adopting my idea, Ms. Warne.

Let's end this fake MAX stop entry with a tribute to Powell's in the form of a haiku:

"A Haiku Tribute to Powell's City of Books"

city block of books
thoughts and people and purpose
possibilities

Galleria/SW 10th Avenue, Day 31

Hey Ms. Warne,

I can't say that I enjoyed my work today. It's a Friday, and Washington County, for some reason, asked me to work a shift from 10 a.m. to 6 p.m.

On a Friday!

Anyway, this threw my day into a little different routine on the MAX both going and coming from work. Luckily, Omar had decided to meet me at work and ride home with me and maybe stop at the L---- Center for a while.

On the way home, three girls that looked about our age got on the MAX. It was very apparent that they were headed somewhere for something BIG because they were all dressed up for something fancy. And I doubt they were headed to Powell's, even though this is one of the nearest stops to get off and walk to my favorite store of all time. Contrary to what Disney would have you think, Powell's really is the happiest place on Earth.

These girls, young women, were full of life and were excitedly talking about wherever they were headed. They were confident and loud, and it was fun to have some fresh, positive enthusiastic vibes on the MAX.

I wasn't the only one who noticed them. There were two older guys sitting just a little past where the three girls were standing. And if I happened to be a superhero named Spider-Man, then my Spidey-sense would have been raging like a class-five rapid on the Deschutes River. Already I could tell something was going to happen.

My mom has done a pretty decent job in helping me understand sexism and how it is still very much a big part of our society. It was on full display here on the MAX.

The two men first started saying things to each other while pointing at the three girls. Then their comments started to get louder, and they weren't positive comments. Then they stood up and walked toward the girls.

"Where are you three lovely ladies going tonight?" one of them said. "Want to have a real good time and come with us instead?"

"No thanks," one of the girls said.

"Oh, come on," one of the guys said, moving in closer to the girls. Too close. The other one moved in closer as well. "The way you're dressed up tells me you're looking for a good time. We're that good time."

The other one laughed, said something under his breath, and made a vulgar gesture.

Then.

"The way they're dressed and where they're going has nothing to do with you," said a voice that was standing up and moving past me.

Omar.

He was walking with purpose toward the men.

"They can dress however they want, and they can go wherever they want, and they can choose whom they want to go with," he said. He used the word "whom," Ms. Warne.

"And I highly recommend you go back to your seats and leave these people alone," he said while getting even closer to the situation. I could see that he was trying to get in between the two guys and the girls.

The fact that somebody was saying something to the two men threw them off for a second or two, but not for long.

"What are you going to do about it, Osama?" Their attention was now on Omar.

I woke up.

And I stood up. And I walked toward Omar and likewise tried to get between them and the girls.

"You heard him," I said. "And you should have heard them," I said pointing at the three girls. "They said they're not interested in having you join them tonight, so leave them alone."

It was tense for about five seconds. The five of us stood there looking defiant.

And thankfully, Ms. Warne . . .

Thankfully, the two men walked away. And got off at the next stop.

When the two men walked away, Omar and I went back to our seats.

"Thanks for saying something," I said to him.

"Why do men have to be such idiots?" Omar asked me. "Why do they act that way?"

His questions made me think about the talks my mom and dad have had with me about sexism, racism, and classism. Especially the sexism and racism I had just seen. Why didn't I stand up before Omar did? Why did it take me longer to do something?

I hate how a lot of boys and men treat girls and women.

We've got to do better, Ms. Warne. We can do better.

PGE Park, Day 32

BART. MAX. CAT. DART.

Hey, Ms. Warne, what do all of these names have in common? You probably guessed it easy enough because I had MAX in that list, and the whole summer I've been writing about the MAX.

I know that all of the big cities don't give names to their mass transit systems (Metro in DC, Subway in NYC, the Tube in London) but a lot of cities do. Why is that? Easy to remember? Research shows that more people will ride if they feel a personal connection to the transportation? "I'm going to take the MAX" versus "I'm going to take the Tube." To quote Shakespeare, "What's in a name," Ms. Warne? Quite a bit actually, at least here in Portland—MAX is so much easier to say than "Metropolitan Area Express."

I started to imagine what it would be like if mass transit got together from all over the world to have a coffee break. Maybe make a cartoon movie of it and call it *Trains* or *In Transit.*

MAX: Hey, BART, how's it going down there in Cali?

BART: Fine, MAX, windy of course. How's your paint job holding up with all that rain?

MAX: Great, they really know how—

Eidan: (breaking in) You slow pathetic examples of mass transit. You can't even get over twenty kilometers per hour. I can go two hundred kilometers per hour.

CATS: (*feline-like-meow sound*)

NORTA: Yeah, well shove it, yah stupid foreigner. At least we're not high strung, shoving people in our doors like they are cattle.

Tube: Hey, now, don't include all non-American rails in this discussion. Your transit system is modeled off my system.

L: Maybe modeled after, but we sure are a heck of a lot better than your old rickety self. And what's with that stupid "Mind the Gap" crap? Who would be dumb enough to leave a gap in the first place?

LYNX: Whoa, everybody. Can't we all get along? We came here for a latte, not to argue.

DART: Yeah, I came here to chat and have a cup of joe, not to listen to all of you bicker.

CATS: (*feline-like-meow sound*)

TRAX: Oh, whatever, DART. We all know why you're really here. You're here 'cause you got the hots for ol' lover girl over there.

MARTA: (bored) Not interested.

Little T: Dad, who is that?

Mr. T: Shut up, kid. I pity the fool. Where's the tea?

Mrs. T: There are children present here, everyone. Can we please stay civil?

SMART: Just because humans can't get along doesn't mean that we can't get along.

SEPTA: Oh, go run yourself off a drawbridge, ya stupid windbag.

CATS: *(feline-like-meow sound)*

MAX: (to BART) Oh, the life of a mass transit car.

BART: You said it, MAXy. You said it.

FART: (scene fades out as we hear him) I think I need a new name . . .

So that you know I didn't make up those names, Ms. Warne, here's a little extra guide:

MAX = Metropolitan Area Express (Portland, Oregon)
BART = Bay Area Rapid Transit (San Franscisco, California)
Eidan = (Tokyo, Japan. I don't speak Japanese)
CATS = Charlotte Area Transit System (Charlotte, North Carolina)
NORTA = New Orleans Regional Transit Authority (New Orleans, Louisiana)
Tube = (London, England. Usually called "the Tube")
L = The L Train. (Chicago, Illinois. I think.)
LYNX = ? (Orlando, Florida)
DART = Dallas Area Rapid Transit (Dallas, Texas)
TRAX = Transit Express (Salt Lake City, Utah)
All the Ts = The T Train. (Chicago, Illinois, I think? Maybe I'm mixing that up with another letter?)
SMART = Sonoma-Marin Area Rapid Transit (Sonoma, California)
FART = Fresno Area Rapid Transit (Fresno, California. I do think the name has been changed. Okay, you caught me, Ms. Warne. This wasn't a real acronym. I just couldn't resist.)

Kings Hill/SW Salmon, Day 33

Ms. Warne,

I'm sorry if I'm starting to sound like the proverbial broken record on this topic, but I just don't get girls/young women/women. As you can see, I don't even know what to refer to them as right now at our age. I sort of consider myself a boy/young man and kind of a man. How should I refer to them? Ask each of them and see what they'd say?

When does a person become an adult? When is a girl not a girl anymore but is a woman?

That question sounds like our discussion from last year when you had us read that chapter from *Winesburg, Ohio* called "Sophistication." I really liked reading that story and talking about it.

The story brought up all sorts of lunchtime conversation from my usual table group. Jay asked why a lot of the academic-type girls seemed to date others who weren't so academically minded. To that musing, Tonya quickly said, "It's fun to date a rebel." Omar then said it would be interesting to see in the future who each of us would seek a relationship with.

Of course, I'm thinking about all of this relationship stuff because of Janie. Why did it seem she was maybe interested in me and then latch onto that guy from J------? Is he a rebel and I'm not?

Why am I interested in a relationship with Janie for that matter? What's motivating me? What's motivating her?

Why do high school students think or feel like we want to have relationships (romantic or otherwise) with other people? Is it instinctual? Societal pressure? Are we seeking sophistication?

Clearly, I'm struggling with this, Ms. Warne. I'm sure you can tell that I've been intentionally writing all sorts of other things the past few days because I'm avoiding what I really want to and need to figure out.

Goose Hollow/SW Jefferson, Day 34

"Meantime, let me ask myself one question—Which is better?—To have surrendered to temptation; listened to passion; made no painful effort—no struggle;—but to have sunk down in the silken snare" (Chapter 31).

"Brothers and Sisters . . ."

Hey, Ms. Warne, the Prophet's back on the MAX.

"The time has come to talk of one thing: choice. Yes, sisters and brothers, choice."

A few people yawned and went back to reading their books or looking out the window. Maybe they'd heard this speech before.

"We can all choose, brothers and sisters. Sometimes we make good choices and sometimes we make bad choices. Today, all of you made a choice to wear what you're wearing. Some of you look good, and others of you don't look as good."

A few people seemed slightly offended, but the majority of the people who were listening gave a wry smile.

"Where does evil come from? Where does good come from? How can you choose good when there's no evil? Choose evil when there's no good? In order to choose one, there must be the other. In order to choose that ugly tie you're wearing" (he pointed at a guy across the way), "you had to have other ties in your closet, right? Otherwise, you had no choice—you were forced to wear that outrageously goofy-looking thing."

"You" (he was now pointing at me again) "choose to work during the summer." At first, Ms. Warne, I was totally surprised when he said this, thinking this guy had been stalking me for the summer, but I realized anyone could know I was working.

I looked like a high school kid going to a summer job.

But then, he said something that really made me wonder about his prophetic skills. Looking at me right in the eyes, he said, "And now you have a big decision to make in the next few days. Choose wisely."

Wow. Me—a big decision to make in the next few days?

Choose wisely? This guy was a mix between the knight sentry in *Indiana Jones* and a fortune cookie. Where were the lottery numbers?

“Choose wisely? About what?” I asked him, but the MAX had stopped and the Prophet was walking out the door. “How do you know I have a choice to make?” I yelled after him.

I don’t know why I even asked him. I already knew the answer. I need to choose wisely about Janie.

I was starting to believe that the Prophet knew the answer as well.

I made up my mind then and there that the next time I saw Janie, I’d ask her about the guy with the J------ jacket. Was this the decision the Prophet was referring to? And if so, how could I know whether or not Janie would be truthful? Is this guy telling me not to go talk with her? I guess I still don’t even know if she likes me or not. Maybe she’s one of those girls who flirt with every single guy they talk to. (I don’t think she is, Ms. Warne, but as you can tell I’m conflicted.)

Washington Park (the Oregon Zoo), Day 35

Hey Ms. Warne,

I never really liked that Simon & Garfunkel song about the zoo. My parents are very big S&G fans and indoctrinated me early on to appreciate their folksy tunes, and I do admit that I generally do like their sound. But that song about "it's all happening at the zoo" always seemed stupid.

Until today.

I don't know what got into me—maybe it was that darn Prophet's words the other day that have been repeating themselves over and over in my mind.

Choose wisely . . . choose wisely . . .

Whatever it was, I made a spur-of-the-moment decision and got off the MAX at the zoo stop. Maybe I had a premonition that something would happen, I don't know.

I had gone to work earlier than usual, so it was around three thirty when I got to the zoo stop, having left work at three. I'm not sure what I really hoped to accomplish, but somehow, I knew that I wanted to get off here and maybe, just maybe, I'd go see Janie. Find out once and for all if there was any chance for "us."

And there's still that issue of what she was writing that day on her laptop. Even if "we" never happen, I'm still curious about what she was writing, because I do think she was hiding something.

I got off the MAX and looked around. I believe it's the only underground stop on the entire Blue Line.

I've never gotten off the MAX here before because my parents and I have only ever come to the zoo via a car. Ms. Warne, if you've not ever come to the zoo via the MAX and checked out the zoo MAX stop, you gotta do it. They have all these crazy cool statues and etchings and sayings. I don't know who made the decision to make this underground MAX stop "scientifically artsy," but I'm impressed. Here were some of the etchings that made me stop and think:

"The universe was created 4,500,000,000 years ago. The sun and earth were formed 4,600,000,000 years ago. Mammals evolved 225,000,000 years ago."

And:

"A seventy-five-foot-long trail of footprints left 3,750,000 years ago in volcanic ash in Africa provides conclusive evidence that our earliest undisputed hominid ancestor, Australopithecus afarensis, walked upright."

And then there's the core sample timeline. This MAX stop is 260 feet underground, and I think it's the deepest rail stop in the United States. When they created this place, and dug down 260 feet, they kept all of the dirt from the top to the bottom. Then, they encased each of the 260 feet of dirt to show how it changed over the past *X* number of years. The last sentence describing the 260 feet of dirt they have encased throughout the stop says:

"Each layer of material was once at the Earth's surface, beginning at a time when things in this area, and throughout the world, were very different from the way they are today."

If we were reading my little book as a class, you'd stop us here and have a discussion now about connecting that quote to the rest of the book and figure out how it's all interconnected. I guess since you're reading this on your own, you'll just have to have that discussion with yourself, or with your pets, if you have any.

Isn't it funny, Ms. Warne? Between last year and this upcoming school year, I will spend one hour a day, five days a week, for roughly seventy-two weeks a year (because it's two years of school) with you in your classroom. That's 360 hours, plus or minus absences for both of us. That's a lot of hours.

How well do you think you know me, Ms. Warne? How well do you think you know any of your students? We know a little about you, and some of it probably isn't accurate, as there is always a lot of kid talk that goes on at schools. We know that your full name is Barbara Mary Warne. Did you know that we sometimes call you BMW or Beemer? We know that you're not married and don't have a boyfriend or girlfriend. Well, I guess we don't really know that, but we don't ever hear you talk about a boyfriend of girlfriend.

That's why you always grade our papers so quickly—you don't have someone else at your house distracting you from what's really important. (That's a joke, although we students do like that you grade our papers quickly.)

You are quirky. And I like that. Some students compare you to Ms. Frizzle from *The Magic School Bus*.

I would like it, too, if you'd tell us more about yourself during class time. And I'm not just saying that to get you to waste time during school so we don't have to do homework. The 360 hours, plus or minus, that we spend with you is more time than some of us spend with our own parents. In some ways, teachers like you have more influence on us than our own moms and dads. Mr. Blanchard was pretty funny when he called himself "another dad" at the beginning of school last year. It's kind of true, though.

Does that thought ever cross your mind? Does it scare you? Empower you?

Sorry, Ms. Warne. That was all very tangential, wasn't it? You probably did what I do when I'm reading a book and it's this really exciting part and then the author decides to put in a bunch of extraneous detail or philosophy or description—I skim until I find the next plot point so I can keep the "real" story going. If you did that (and I don't really blame you) then you can start reading again HERE.

I spent way too long looking at and thinking about the zoo MAX stop, and I talked myself out of actually going up the elevator. Lots of second thoughts here about fooling myself and thinking that something might really be there between me and Janie.

I boarded the next MAX and went home.

Washington Park (the Oregon Zoo Part 2), Day 36

Ms. Warne,

Yes, a break in the structure of my little summer project. Two stops at the zoo. One yesterday and another today.

I spent most of last night thinking about what the Prophet said to me about choice and decisions. And I talked myself back into trying to talk to Janie.

This time I didn't stop and ponder on the deepness of the zoo art, but instead left sixteen million years ago and went up the elevator to the Present. (That's what some clever person named the two levels here at the transit stop. How cool is that? The lower level is sixteen million years ago and 260 feet later in an elevator ride is the Present.)

I went into the zoo.

This was also somewhat interesting. Did you wonder how I got into the zoo? I guess I could leave that little detail to you, my teacher-reader, to just wonder about or not, but it's a little more complicated than it might seem. I don't carry cash, and last night I had left my debit card out on my dresser and forgot to put it back in my wallet when I left this morning. When I got to the zoo entrance and opened my wallet, I realized my stupid mistake, only to luckily find my parent's zoo membership pass wedged in between two receipts. (Hey, if Hamlet could just "happen" to have his dead dad's ring in his pocket while on a pirate ship, why is it so unlikely that I'd have a zoo pass?)

Once in the zoo, however, reality again came crashing down upon me. I had no clue where Janie might be. The zoo is a big place and the likelihood of me roaming around and just bumping into her was probably 1 in 45,430. But then . . . a voice.

"Hey, Ty."

It wasn't her.

It was Grant May, another kid from our school. He had on a ZooTeen shirt. At school he has the reputation of being smart and a little eccentric.

"Hey, Grant," I said. "You volunteering here this summer?"

"Yeah. What are you doing here?"

"Uh . . ." What do I say to this guy?

He didn't give me a chance.

“Janie told us all about your rap. I’m working with the Madagascar hissing cockroaches today—do you think you’d rap for them? I think they’d really like it. Their hissing might add to your sound.”

Madagascar hissing cockroaches?

“Probably not today, Grant,” I said. “Maybe another time.” And then, “Hey, where is Janie?” That was pretty slick, eh, Ms. Warne?

“She’s usually with the otters, but she’s not here today. She volunteers every day except Thursdays and Sundays. Are you sure you can’t rap for the Madagascar hissing cockroaches?”

“Sorry, Grant, I gotta go. See you around.”

Well, Ms. Warne, what do I do next? What do I do now?

I can come back here again.

I can wait until I see her on the MAX again.

I can just leave it all alone.

All alone.

Sunset Transit Center, Day 37

Ms. Warne,

As most experienced MAX riders know, there are four coveted seats on every train. Those are the four seats at the front and back of the train that face the opposite direction that the train is going and the opposite way of the rest of the people.

In other words, you don't have to look at other people, and you don't have to have other people looking at you. This is the closest thing to "privacy" that a person can have on the MAX—in essence, when you sit in these seats, you're sending a not-so-subliminal message to the rest of the ridership that you don't want to engage with them.

Everybody understands this and everybody is cool with it.

However.

There is one drawback to sitting in these sought-after seats, as I found out today.

Since I get on the MAX early in the morning and it's at Cleveland Avenue, I usually get my pick of whatever seat I want to ride in for the next hour and a half. Often, I choose the "private" seat because I want to read and write and be anti-social like the rest of the passengers. Sitting forward, pretty much oblivious to everyone else getting on, I found myself dozing off. Eventually, several stops later, I woke up with the sense that someone had sat in the seat directly behind me, facing the other way. But the person, whoever she was, was talking like she had her head turned and was talking or whispering to the back of my head.

"I had Jesus over at my house last night," she said. "Jesus, Jesus, Jesus. He was over last night."

Ms. Warne, I know there are some people that ride the MAX that maybe have some mental health struggles, so I didn't think much of this, except it sounded like she was talking directly to me. What made it worse was that I couldn't see who was saying it. I didn't want to cause problems by turning around and saying, "Hi. Are you talking to me?" I also admit that I was kind of scared. What would happen if I turned around and tried to talk with her?

"Jesus is my friend," she continued, this time quieter and softer. "But last night he was mean, so I had to leave. Jesus, Jesus, Jesus, Jesus. Had to leave Jesus, so I walked on out."

Then, she started to cry a little.

"Now I need to find a new friend. I need a new friend. No more Jesus. I need a new friend. Will you please be my friend?"

Was she talking to me? Do I dare turn around and look and see who is saying all of this? What if I turn around? What's the best thing to do here? Will she yell at me if I try to talk to her?

Hoping for the best, I continued staring straight ahead, praying that this person behind me was just someone who regularly talks to herself.

"Yes, Jesus called me on the phone last night and then he came over. He wanted to save my soul, but I was mad because he was mean. So, I didn't let him save my soul. And then he left. And now I'm . . ."

Could anybody else hear this woman? Why didn't someone else say something to her?

Still, I couldn't turn around and look at her. I was frozen from inaction.

The MAX stopped.

I thought about turning around, I thought about jumping out of my seat and making a run for the doors, and I did think about starting a conversation, but the talking stopped.

The talking *stopped.*

I assumed she got off the train, since the talking had stopped, so I slowly inched my head around and . . . saw that the seat was empty.

Ms. Warne, you know when we read that book *Of Mice and Men* and we talked about how that one guy regretted not taking care of his own dog but allowed someone else to? That's how I feel now about not talking with this person—I won't go so far to say I'm haunted by her, but I do find myself wondering who she is and what she looks like.

Will I see her again and not realize it?

Does she ride the MAX everyday like me?

I should (using it here, because I am shaming myself) have looked to see who it was. I need to not be scared or afraid and do nothing. Especially for people who may need help or may be without a home or may just need a friendly hello. It's just not that hard. And as I've said before, this summer is teaching me that I can do hard things.

I'm not going to sit in the "private" seats anymore.

Beaverton Transit Center, Day 38

"Was I very gleeful, settled, content, during the hours I passed in yonder bare, humble school-room this morning and afternoon? Not to deceive myself, I must reply—No: I felt desolate to a degree" (Chapter 33).

Hey Ms. Warne,

I'm sitting here, not able to read *Jane Eyre*, mostly because I'm thinking about Janie and mulling over what I'm going to do or not going to do. I'm still not doing anything, as you probably can tell.

I'm watching three other kids my age that get on the MAX, so of course I check out what they're doing. They all have phones out, and all three of them are texting.

I hope they're not texting each other.

If you've made it this far in my little summer assignment, you might be asking yourself, "Where is this kid's cell phone? Why doesn't he just call or text Janie?"

I have a phone, Ms. Warne, but it's not a cool phone. It's a dumb phone and all I can do is make phone calls with it. And I'm fine with that. I really don't like talking on the phone, and I really doubt I would like texting. Give me a real, open, honest, live conversation and I'm all good.

And I'm not the only one either who feels this way. Remember when you tried that Internet-based program in class where we could write our opinion on our phone and it would be displayed on the screen through your projector? I wasn't the only one in class that didn't have a smartphone. In fact, I think there were only fifteen of the thirty-two of us that did have one, so your lesson was kind of a dud (sorry for the honesty there).

I'm going to ask you a question, Ms. Warne, and even if you don't read any of the rest of this summer assignment (I know how you teachers work—reading a little bit of our work to make us think you really read the whole thing) I want your honest opinion about this question.

What do you think of my generation?

You can use the margins to write some of your thoughts down with your famous purple gel pen.

Really, I'd like to know what you think about us. I'm not so naïve to assume that we are the greatest generation to come along in sixty years. But then again, we're not really that terrible either.

I know we've been referred to as "Gen-whatever," "the Apathetic Generation," or "Gen Why?" but I think those are all unfair.

Yes, we are becoming products of our society, and yes, MANY may be somewhat out of control with the need for "our technology." (Like I said, not me—I am happy with just having a dumb phone.)

But what generation hasn't had its indulgences? Rock 'n' roll, drugs, shirts with lions, cars—you name it, every generation has had something that previous generations frowned upon. At least we're not "lost" like those people from *The Sun Also Rises* that we read about in class two years ago.

Where have we learned this so-called phenomenon of apathy? Why does everyone want a new phone? Why is it easier to text than to talk on the phone or hang out? When did where we are at "today" begin? Who is to blame? Us? Previous generations? Things fall apart, Ms. Warne, right? There's no one specific event that causes a generation to be the way it is—we are a product of previous generations who were products of previous generations and so on and so on and so on . . . all the way to 3,750,000 years ago, right?

Personally, I get so tired of adults going off on my generation. We need more role models and fewer critics. What we've learned, we've learned by watching you, all right? (Not you personally, Ms. Warne, no personal attack there. I was just having fun using a line from that famous anti-drug commercial.)

We will grow up and be productive, contributing members of society. We aren't going to ruin our country or society or our cultures any more than any other previous generation has done.

End of rant.

Beaverton Central, Day 39

Hi Ms. Warne,

Still in a bit of a rut/funk today when we pulled up to BC. I glanced out the window and saw him.

The Prophet.

He was standing outside holding up a huge digital clock of some kind. It was counting down—right then it was at thirty, twenty-nine, twenty-eight, and my curiosity got the best of me, so I scurried off the MAX to see what might happen when the clock got down to zero.

Some other curious-minded individuals had also gathered around to see what was going to happen when time ran out. Was the world going to end? Would the Prophet discourse on something profound? Maybe he'd have some more advice that would help me make a decision about Janie.

Five . . . four . . . three . . . two . . . one . . . zero

"The time has come to talk of one thing, sisters and brothers." There were about ten of us gathered around him by now.

"Country music." He pulled out a cowboy hat from what seemed like thin air and put it on his head.

Country music? A cowboy hat? The Prophet?

You gotta be kidding me. The Prophet is going to talk about country music? I'm needing/hoping/expecting some life-changing insights because I'm in a bad way, and this guy's going to extrapolate on country music?

Some of the others must have been thinking the same thing because there were some laughs and a few people left.

"Yes, brothers and sisters, country music."

I don't think I've told you before, Ms. Warne, but I really don't like country music. I'm pretty eclectic in my musical-listening repertoire, but country music has just never impressed me.

"Everything anyone needs to know about life and existence can be learned from country music," the Prophet was saying.

"I've got friends in low places, but love can still be deeper than a holler. And though there's a tear in your beer, I will always love you."

Some of the others standing around with me (mostly older people) were smiling and clearly were amused—they were getting something out of this meaningless rambling.

But I didn't get it.

"The red dirt road always leads to a ring of fire where you and I go fishing in the dark. If tomorrow never comes, I need you now, because rain is a good thing." The next MAX was pulling in, and I'd heard enough, so I started to walk away.

"Country roads take me home because I'm gonna stand by your man before he cheats something fancy."

I started to get on the MAX.

"Yes, sisters and brothers, country music will set you free—"

The doors closed and I couldn't hear the Prophet anymore.

And it didn't matter.

He wasn't helping me anyway.

Millikan Way, Day 40

Pressured. Overwhelmed. Hurried. Rushed. Despondent. This is how i feel.

Ms. Warne,

I know my troubles and difficulties are nothing when compared to kids my own age in places where they don't know where their next meal is coming from, but that doesn't mean that the way I feel isn't real.

I am downtrodden. That's the best word I can come up with to describe how I feel right now. I don't want to use the word depressed because I know kids that have real depression, and that's not me. But I am definitely out of sorts.

Maybe downtrodden isn't the perfect word for how I feel, but it's mostly how I feel. Just bleh. Or blah. Just this sense of anxiety and futility and pressure all wrapped up into one giant feeling of blah. Or bleh.

I know everyone gets this feeling at least occasionally because I've heard my mom and dad talk about it when they've felt it. I know they had it really bad when Dom died. I guess I could say that I've seen it manifest itself as well at my house—when one of us has the blahs, the others know it. I've seen movies about serious blahs too—like big-time depression, so I know it's a real thing.

I have no *major* reason to feel this way, and like all of the other times in my life when I feel this way, it seems to work itself out of my system in a day or two and I'm back to feeling not so down anymore. I'll be back to feeling "normal," whatever that means. I guess normal means back to feeling how I feel most of the time, which constitutes normalcy or the feeling I have regularly.

Like I said, I know everyone has good days and bad days, and I guess today's just another of my bad days. What's a little tough is I've had a few bad days in a row and that's hard. Usually, the bad days come about because several things happen all at once rather than spreading themselves out over the course of a few weeks so they seem more manageable.

I'm not going to go into the four of five things weighing me down (and they're not huge), but I guess I just want you to know that I'm human and I worry and get down in the clichéic dumps every now and then.

I worry about my future.

I worry about my grades.

I worry about whether or not there's really life after death. (Don't worry, Ms. Warne, you don't need to talk to my school counselor.)

I worry about whether or not I should talk to Janie.

I think a lot about Janie.

And I think a lot about purpose.

My purpose.

I don't think I'm excessively consumed with these feelings either, Ms. Warne. Like I said, everyone sometimes feels like they just don't want to do anything. I do think most kids my age worry occasionally about these things (or even bigger struggles they have).

Well, maybe I do think more about this stuff than other kids—I scored a ten-out-of-ten on that existential thing that dealt with multiple intelligences that we did in Advisory my freshman year.

I feel bad for those people who get the blahs and can't ever break free from them. That would be tough. Most of us feel them for a few hours or a day or two, realize we're in a funk (as my mom calls it), and then we are luckily able to work through it. People with depression—they're the ones that have it tougher. Those and kids from places that worry every day if they'll live to wake up in the morning.

What I guess I'm getting at, Ms. Warne, is that I'm struggling. And so are a lot of other people. I know as my dad has taught me that comparison is the thief of joy, but I'm going to compare here anyway, and remind myself that while my struggles are real, they're not as complex as a lot of other people's struggles.

I can do this.

Beaverton Creek, Day 41

Ms. Warne,

Trouble today on the MAX, and I mean trouble with a capital *T* and that rhymes with *P* and that stands for people.

People with knives to be exact.

The MAX is safe.

I feel very safe while riding. It's just like school though. Every now and then, when you put hundreds of people together in small, cramped quarters, tempers will fly and somebody will get hurt.

I'm still sort of in a funk, but I'd pulled myself out enough to be reading *Jane Eyre*, knowing that I've got to keep pushing through.

And then, in front of me, a way down the aisle, two guys started getting in each other's faces and were posturing like something was going to go down real soon. A little pushing ensued, and then, in what seemed like a magician's trick, a knife appeared in one of the two men's hands.

Once that knife was out, the other man brandished one as well, and at this point, I knew this wasn't going to go well for one and all.

I was scared, but I have learned my lesson, and I quickly reached over and pushed the emergency button and said into the speaker as quietly and urgently as I could, "There's two guys fighting and they have knives." (I didn't want them to hear me as I didn't want them to come after me.)

The MAX screeched to a stop and the two men were temporarily thrown off balance. I saw the MAX police running toward our train car where the doors were going to open and let the security get things under control.

But they didn't get there quite in time.

When the two men were thrown off balance from the braking train, one of them reoriented himself faster than the other, and was able to swipe once at the other guy. His knife found skin on the other guy's arm when the guy tried to block the attack.

I've never seen a knife fight before and I hope I never do again. I didn't lose my breakfast because (a) I hadn't eaten anything before I got on the train (think Honey Bunches of Oats), and (b) I had previously at least seen a flesh wound like that when my left calf was cut open by an opposing football player's cleats two years ago.

When that had happened, I felt something like a scratch on my leg, but when I looked, there was a four-inch gash all the way down to fat and muscle. I'd never seen my own fat and muscle, and I don't know why, but it didn't hurt, and all I said as I walked over the sideline was, "Coach, I think I need a Band-Aid."

Anyway, I didn't lose my breakfast even though the knife wound looked like it was all the way to muscle and fat like my football wound. I still have that scar by the way, Ms. Warne. Let me know if you ever want to see it.

The doors opened and security grabbed the two men, physically hauled them off in different directions, and once again the train was quiet.

Nobody had gathered around and made a ring around these two men, Ms. Warne.

Nobody.

I guess maybe it's not exactly like high school after all.

Merlo/SW 158th Avenue, Day 42

Ms. Warne,

After yesterday's scary scene, I will admit I'm a little jittery about riding the MAX again.

But even though I'm riding again, I'm not going to do anything.

Just sit.

And watch.

And be careful.

Elmonica/SW 170th Avenue, Day 43

Ms. Warne,

I admit it. I am just wasting my time.

I've got no motivation and nothing comes from nothing, which is about twice as much energy as I've got these days.

I was so bored and so apathetic that I wrote a really stupid poem. Here it is:

"The Caveman"

There once was a caveman named Glug,
Who looked very close to a slug.
He was ugly and hairy,
he wasn't named Larry,
And all he could say was "zug zug."

Glug's girlfriend's name was Crudla,
She was real squat and ate foodla.
When they had a date,
It was Gluggie's fate
To be bonked on the head with a clubla.

Glug went and invented the fire.
And this is how; I'm no liar.
His breath was so bad,
He burped what he had,
And behold a flame in the mire.

The rest of his life was a flop.
He'd eat dino until he would drop.
The Ice Age then came,
Glug wasn't the same,
And now he's a frozen cream pop.

End of the poem, Ms. Warne. Thankfully, huh?

What am I doing? I've got to pull myself together.

Willow Creek/SW 185th Transit Center, Day 44

Ms. Warne,

Some parents got onto the MAX today with their little kids. I think they were both boys around the age of three or four.

And they both had sticks.

Boys with sticks.

I smiled because I've long had the idea to write a kid's book called *Boys with Sticks* and have pictures of various boys playing with sticks.

"What's so novel about that?" you might ask me, Ms. Warne.

Let me tell you.

You ever watched boys play outside at a park or in a forest? What's bound to happen sooner rather than later?

You got it—the boys will pick up sticks and play with them
or throw them
or hit things with them
or just carry them around

It's like it's part of little kids' DNA to gravitate to sticks and *have to* do something with them.

It's only been lately (especially after that Gulf War guy came into our class) that I've developed an idea for the final page of my kid's book, which really wouldn't be a kid's book anymore if I put this final image into it.

The final page for my *Boys with Sticks* book would be a soldier holding a gun.

Just another boy with a stick, Ms. Warne.

Quatama/NW 205th Avenue, Day 45

"Brother."

"Brother."

"The time has come."

Ms. Warne,

I had kind of fallen asleep when I felt someone sit next to me and nudge me a little to wake me up. And those were the words he spoke to me.

He was sitting next to me.

And he was talking to me.

"Brother, the time has come to talk of one thing."

"Love."

"Yes, my brother, love."

Lest there be any doubt about who he was talking to, he looked straight at me and said, "Yeah, I'm talking to you, so just listen to what I have to say."

His voice sounded different from how it usually sounded—maybe because he was right next to me using his little Prophetic voice rather than his big Prophetic voice.

"Okay. I'll listen," I said.

"Love is the strongest force in the world," he said, "and if you don't ever take a chance to give that love a chance, you won't ever feel what it is that causes this great big round ball of ours to spin."

He paused.

"You might be scared to give it a shot, but if you don't try it on for size, you'll never know if it fits or not. You'll never know what you missed out on."

Pause again.

"And that's a shame."

He looked at me square in the face and said, "Quit wasting your hours and days. Quit writing stupid poems about cavemen. And don't give up, Ty."

And then he got up and glided out the open doors of the MAX without even looking around.

How did he know my name, Ms. Warne?
How did he know my name?
And how does he know about me and Janie?

Washington Park (the Oregon Zoo Part 3), Day 46

Hey Ms. Warne,

Cliché alert: Hopefully, the third time's the charm. And, yes, I know this MAX stop chapter of mine is completely out of order, but I headed back again to the zoo. After listening to the Prophet, I knew I had to do it.

It was like his little pep talk had snapped me out the funk I was in and helped me realize what I needed to do.

I once again left 16,000,000 years ago, rode up the elevator, and landed in the Present.

Thanks to Grant's tidbit of information from before, I headed straight to the otters.

There she was.

I saw Janie.

She saw me.

She didn't look surprised at all.

"Hey," I said.

"Hi. I kinda thought you might show up here," she said.

The dazed and confused look on my face must have prompted her next words. "Grant told me you came last week."

"Oh, yeah, Grant . . ." I said. "Madagascar hissing cockroaches."

She smiled.

"I'm on break. You want to go for a walk?"

"Sure."

We started walking.

"So, how's it been? I haven't seen you in a while. You still riding the MAX every day?"

"Every day," I said. "And you? How's the zoo?"

"Great. I really like it here."

No time like the present, Ms. Warne.

"I'm still curious about what you were writing on the MAX the other day."

"Is that why you're here?"

Choose wisely.

"Sort of."

"Sort of?"

"Partially."

"Partially?" Her voice was playful as she then said, "I told you that if we saw each other twice more I'd show you what I wrote. Even if you count today as one of two, there's still one more—"

"I saw you last week as well." I sort of, well, mostly, cut her off just to get it out in the open because I sensed this was a critical do-or-die moment. "You were with some guy from J-------. I think you saw me too."

Even though I was trying to maintain an even, calm tone while mentioning the guy from J-------, I don't think it worked very well because my hurt and jealousy must have tipped Janie off about how I was feeling.

Janie knew what I was talking about.

"I didn't see you, but you . . . you saw me with Sam and he had his arm around me . . ." she trailed off.

Sam.

Sam that goes to school at J--------.

Then Janie smiled.

"He's a ZooTeen volunteer too. He was goofing around. You saw him when he was imitating some guy at his school that was trying to be suave with a coworker." She laughed.

"And . . . you . . . you thought he was my boyfriend . . ."

"Yes."

"And you came here to ask me about that."

Choose wisely.

Second (or third?) moment of truth, Ms. Warne.

"Yes."

And then I added: "I'm actually hoping you don't have a boyfriend."

If this was a chick flick or a rom-com, Ms. Warne, we would have, at that moment, leaned toward each other and music would swell and romantic inclinations would fill the hearts and souls of everyone in the movie theater.

But this is not a chick flick nor a rom-com. This is 20-- and this is real life.

Before she could say anything, someone yelled, "Janie!" across the way and another girl our age was running toward us. "Janie, Dr. Curtiss needs you right now—she's giving Trixie and Nixie some shots and things aren't going well."

"I gotta go," she said. She started hurrying away with the other girl, but stopped long enough to say, "Ty, I'll count this as another time we met. The next time I see you, and I do want to see you, I'll let you read what I was writing."

Orenco/NW 213th Avenue, Day 47

Dear Mr. Rochester,

(Another letter to a character in the book, Ms. Warne.)

You don't know me—my name is Ty Clark.

I'm reading Charlotte Brontë's book called *Jane Eyre* and you're in it.

You just got dumped by Jane because you are still married to that person that lives upstairs.

I gotta admit, I've grown to like Jane and I think she made the right decision to not run away with you. When she said, "Mr. Rochester, I will *not* be yours," in chapter 27 I was impressed, to say the least.

Like you, I'm also currently trying to figure out my next steps in a relationship. You were pretty good about taking the breakup, being all gentle and kind with Jane even though I'm sure you wanted to yell at her. Good job.

And then you just disappear from the book. Jane runs away that night and you're gone. I'm not done reading the story yet, so maybe you come back, but maybe you don't. I'll find out in the next couple of days.

What are you doing and thinking right now when you're not in the book? Hanging out? Checking on your wife to make sure she's okay? Pining away? Writing poems about cavemen? Spending more time with Adèle? That's what I think you ought to be doing.

Since you're not really busy right now, maybe you can give me some advice. I'm still the main character of my own story, and I'm not disappearing like you, so what next? What do you recommend I do next?

What's that?

Have patience?

That's it? That's all you got for me? Nothing profound?

When I wrote a letter to Jane, she at least had a question for me to think about. You got any questions for me that might help me work this out in my head?

Wait for it?

That's not a question. Wait for what?

Hawthorn Farm, Day 48

Ms. Warne,

Nothing really interesting happened yesterday. That's why I wrote a letter to Mr. Rochester. I almost left the page blank to see what you'd do. Would that have thrown you off? Would it make you wonder if I messed up? Would you turn the page back and forth and back and forth and wonder, "Ty, what happened? Are you struggling because of what happened yesterday?"

Maybe you would just think that my printer ran out of ink.

Or that I'm getting bored with writing about every day so I just skipped a page.

Or maybe it would cause you to wonder if I've been making this entire thing up and I'm just now typing whatever comes to mind because it's actually the day before school starts and it's due tomorrow and I'm running out of time and I'm out of good ideas of what happened over my summer.

Or any number of other possibilities.

Any or all of them or none of them could be true at any given point, right?

I'll answer my own question.

Right.

The answer that's true is that I'm writing every day about what happens on the MAX and what I've been thinking about while riding the MAX. Or about *Jane Eyre*.

Just so you know, Mr. Rochester didn't really tell me to be patient. I made that up myself.

Here's what happened today.

A woman boarded the MAX with a baby cow following her on a leash.

Yes, you read that correctly—she had a baby cow following her onto the MAX.

She led the baby cow nearby to where I was sitting, so that my head was basically at the same level as the cow's. It looked at me and I have to admit, I was struck.

Struck by the beauty of the cow's eyes.

You ever look at a cow's eyes, Ms. Warne? They're huge . . . and beautiful.

I know that sounds ridiculous, especially when you remember that I was sitting on a train that runs through Portland and I was looking directly into the face of a baby cow.

Besides being huge, this cow's eyes were bright and shiny and looked like glass. They looked like I could see right into the cow's soul and the cow could see into mine.

The other passengers thought it was very cute that a baby cow was on the MAX—they all came over and asked the owner if they could pet the baby cow, which they did.

I did not pet the cow—I was too busy wondering what the cow was wondering about.

Keep Portland Weird, Ms. Warne. Keep it weird.

Fair Complex/Hillsboro Airport, Day 49

Ms. Warne,

I'm going to elaborate a little more on yesterday's topic. The one I was writing about before the baby cow boarded the MAX.

How do you know whether or not what I'm turning in to you as my assignment actually happened? Can your teacher-sense tell you if what I'm writing every day as I ride the MAX is true or not? Or does it not matter to you as long as it's interesting and well written and not boring?

I hope this hasn't been boring.

What if some of what I've been writing has happened and some of it is fiction? What if what actually happened didn't happen, and what you think I made up is what actually is true? (The part about me trying to help the woman have her baby really did happen, Ms. Warne, in case you're questioning that.)

I didn't sleep much last night, as my mind has been going a million miles an hour. I can't stop thinking about Janie and what happened yesterday. The next time I see her, she'll tell me what she was writing on her laptop.

You know, now that I'm thinking about this, it really makes no sense. Why is it even important what she was writing on her laptop? Why has that become the driving point of our conversations and interactions? I really ought to just focus on the here and now of who she is and what our relationship might become.

I'm laughing out loud as I write this because I can hear you in class saying, "What is the dramatic question of this story? What drives the action of the novel?" Clearly, for my silly little summer assignment, it's becoming, "What was Janie writing?"

Or, for the romantics out there, it might be, "Will Ty and Janie get together?"

What do you want to happen, Ms. Warne?

I've got a couple days left of riding the MAX—a couple of days for the rest of this story to unfold. Are you cheering for me, hoping Janie and I will meet again and all will be revealed? Or do you not like tidy, happy little endings where all of the Dickensian setups and payoffs are accounted for? You are an English teacher, after all. And the word on the street is that English teachers all prefer realistic, unhappy endings where the author really hasn't tied up all of the loose ends because that's how life is: untidy with loose ends. Messy.

Since you're not here, and since everything I've told you has actually happened (or has it? Ha ha, thank you Tim O'Brien and *The Things They Carried*!), I guess you're just going to have to be led along like all readers of books. Powerless to the decisions of authors and where they choose to go with the story.

But then again—now that I think about this, I too am sort of being swept along with how this story is going to end.

I don't know if I'm going to see Janie again. I don't know what she was writing on her laptop. I don't know if we're going to get together. If this were a Stephen King book, we'd all be hurtling headlong toward a really unrealistic, may I say, stupid ending. (A spider from outer space? Really?) No offense to Mr. King, who is a brilliant writer, but his endings . . .

I hope my summer story isn't heading that way. I guess you and I will find out—I over the next week, and you over the next ten minutes if you keep reading. Kind of crazy to think that I actually have to live through all of this and you can breeze through it in no time at all, or even skip ahead and find out how this all ends. Do you ever wish you could skip ahead in real life and find out what happens?

That's how I feel right now.

Washington/SE 12th Avenue, Day 50

"'Show me, show me the path!' I entreated of Heaven. I was excited more than I had ever been; and whether what followed was the effect of excitement, the reader shall judge" (Chapter 41).

Ms. Warne,

I had just reread that passage in *Jane Eyre* and the subsequent supernatural gothic voice from nowhere telling Jane to return to Mr. Rochester when my phone rang. Brontë's voice from nowhere is a bit contrived, but it's not as bad as an alien spider.

But yes, you read it right. My phone.

The thing that I hardly ever use.

It rang.

I set down my book, got the phone out of my pocket, and answered: "Hello?"

"Go back to the zoo."

Even though I knew whose voice was on the other end, I still said, "Who is this?"

"Ty . . . go back to the zoo. Now."

Click.

The Prophet hung up on me.

Discarding all common sense, ignoring the fact that I would likely miss work, and certainly not even questioning the fact that a complete stranger somehow had my phone number and called me (knowing where I was too), I got off the MAX and stepped right back on. This time on the train going the other way back toward the zoo.

I admit, Ms. Warne, that for a few short minutes, I was wondering if I had somehow been transported into *Jane Eyre* and when I reached the zoo—that it would have burned down and Janie would be blind. No joke. My head was reeling and I questioned if I was losing my sense of reality.

The MAX slowed down, stopped at 260 feet below ground, and I got off.

And there stood Janie.

And she wasn't blind.

But she did have a huge swath of bandages covering her right hand and it was pretty apparent that she was in pain.

She didn't see me at first, and I walked slowly toward her. When she saw me, and I was by her side, she smiled a little. "Fancy meeting you here," she said.

And then she reached out her left hand, took my right hand in hers, and said, "Is it okay if I hold your hand and you go with me to the hospital? I could use a little help right now. I'm not feeling super steady."

I was more than willing to oblige her, not going to lie here, Ms. Warne.

"What happened?" I asked.

The MAX pulled up, the doors opened, and we walked inside and sat down.

For the next few minutes, Janie relayed the story to me. It was all about an otter fight (Nixie and Trixie) and Janie trying to help separate them when both of them decided to turn on her. Her right hand got scratched, clawed up, and bitten several times.

"The zoo is having me go to Tuality Hospital to have everything checked out," she concluded. "I'll probably have to get a tetanus shot too."

"Are your parents going to come meet you at the hospital?" I asked.

Pause.

"My parents? Oh . . . the zoo . . . tried to call them . . . but they weren't home . . . Yeah, so the zoo people said for me to go on my own." I chalked up her pauses and hesitations to the shock of the otter bites, but something seemed a little out of place in her explanation.

And then she asked pretty quickly, as if to change the subject, "Aren't you supposed to be at work? What were you doing coming to the zoo from the other direction?"

It was my turn to smile a little now.

"What do you know about the archaic definition of the word weird?"

Tuality Hospital/SE 8th Avenue, Still Day 50

Ms. Warne,

Janie and I walked the short distance from the MAX to Tuality Hospital where Janie checked in with the receptionist.

"Ah, yes, you're the one the zoo called about. Have a seat. A doctor will visit with you shortly."

On the walk to the hospital, she didn't say much. I relayed to her the improbable, highly unlikely, too-fictional-to-be-nonfiction story about my phone ringing and the Prophet telling me to go back to the zoo.

As we sat down in the waiting room of the hospital, she said, "It's kind of hard to believe."

She paused.

"But I believe it."

I think we were both a little in shock about what had happened and what was happening. Surreal wouldn't even start to describe everything that was going on. We were both quiet for a minute, and then she said, opening her backpack, "I promised you that the next time we met this summer, you could read what I was writing that day back in June."

I started to protest, mostly because she had let go of my hand to get into her backpack. "I don't need to read it right now—" I started to say.

"It's the right time, Ty," she said.

She opened up the laptop, typed in her password, and started to hand it to me.

A nurse interrupted: "Are you Janie? The doctor will see you now."

She handed me the laptop. "You can read it while I'm gone."

Tuality Hospital (In the Waiting Area), Still Day 50

Here's what i read, Ms. Warne—it started off with a poem Janie wrote called "The Front Porch."

Silently sitting on my porch steps
watching the stars twirl—
watching the pale, empty moon move across the sky,
I feel lonely and quiet, yet I am content.
Content because the night is calm, placid—almost liquid.
But alone because no one shares this moment with me.
If only I could share this feeling with someone—
talk with them—stroll with them
listen to their teeth chatter and
share this brisk evening with them.
The peace I feel on this chill night
Alone is too much for me to carry.
Won't you come and join me in my solitude?
I'll save a spot for you on
my front porch.

It's been almost a year now that I've been at this new high school and I still haven't made very many friends. Transitions are always hard and I hate how often the transitions have had to happen. Life in the foster system really sucks sometimes.

I get so angry at my biological parents for what they did to each other. And to me. And I feel like I've been dealt a bad hand of cards whenever I think about the choices they made and how their actions have permanently scarred me. Sometimes I just want to scream—other times I just want to curl up in a ball and tell the world to stop because I want to get off.

I do have to say that writing about it helps. I'm glad my caseworker helped me get into writing and then into reading, as both of them are ways for me to try to escape or cope with all of the baggage that this weary traveler carries with her.

I'm playing around with poetry too, but it's not very good. It's mostly me throwing my thoughts and wishes around in short little lines.

Like that poem I wrote last night while sitting on my porch—not great, but it gets my feelings out and helps me think through stuff.

I do wish I had someone to talk to. Someone my age I could trust enough to share what's happened to me and what's made me who I am. It's just so hard at school to find someone who I think will take me as is and not just the honor-student kid that I'm trying to be and will listen to me and still like me even though I'm damaged.

That's a strong word, but it's how I feel a lot of the time. I'm a damaged kid with a sh----- past trying to break free.

I put on a good show. I don't think that anyone at the school really knows that I don't live with my bio parents. I just call my foster parents "my parents" and nobody knows any different. Maybe Ms. Warne knows, 'cause she's a teacher, and I might have written something that made her look up my file, but other than her, everyone thinks I'm like everyone else, taking hard classes and volunteering and then going to college.

There is one boy at school that I would really like to talk to. His name is Ty. I know I sound like a stalker, but when I've seen him at school, I just get the sense that he might listen to me and maybe we could understand each other and maybe hang out. I know he likes books because he hangs around Ms. Warne's class all of the time, so he must be an okay guy, right? Boys who read a lot of books have got to have some depth to them, right . . . ? Hopefully . . . ?

It doesn't hurt that Ty is kind of cute, too.

But then, what are the chances that he'd like me and listen to me and not judge me? That's what always keeps me from talking to him or really anyone else for that matter.

I'm just ruined, plain Janie in the foster system and he's probably never had a problem in his life and he's . . .

he's sitting right over there across from me as I type this.

Back to me (Ty) now, Ms. Warne.

I slowly closed Janie's laptop, and sat there, stunned.

Foster kid?

Baggage?
Damaged?
Ruined?
Permanently scarred?

She thinks I'm kind of cute? That certainly made my heart beat faster, but what does "kind of" mean?

Never in my life would I have imagined that I would find myself liking (or loving?) a person who would have described herself with those words.

A foster kid.
Baggage.
Damaged.
Ruined.
Permanently scarred.

Please don't judge me, Ms. Warne, but you gotta remember that even though my parents have done a good job bringing me up and teaching me about all of the isms, this revelation about Janie's past still shocked me to the core because she suddenly wasn't at all who I thought she might be.

Could I really be that person Janie described? That she thought I might be like? Could I talk with her and listen to her and have a lot of fun with her even now that I knew what she'd experienced? What did her parents do to her?

I sat there for ten minutes.

Then twenty.

And then I walked out of the hospital and never went back.

Just kidding—that would be the kind of ending you English teachers like.

I sat there for thirty minutes.

What was I going to say to her when she came out? What was she going to say? What's going to happen in the next thirty minutes?

Every time a door opened, my heart would race and then it wouldn't be her. Was she going to be okay? Why was it taking so long? Was she hurt worse than she let on before? Were otter bites possibly fatal? That sounded really silly writing it out, but it was a thought I had.

By the time the door opened an hour later, and I saw her come out with an even bigger bandage covering her hand, I knew I had the answer to the question of whether or not I could care for this person.

I have never felt that way for anyone like I felt at that moment. It is so indescribable that I won't even try to describe it.

As I stood up and she walked toward me, feeling the way I did, I started to cry. Not hysterically and not out of control—just little tears that I'd not felt on my face since my brother had died.

"Are you okay?" I quietly said.

"Yes."

My crying probably made it awkward, and she said, "What did you think of what I wrote?"

There was a long pause and looking back, I bet it made Janie worry about my response.

I know, Ms. Warne—thanks to my mom's and dad's dinner-time talks—that I should always ask for permission before touching a girl, but I had no words then that could convey how I felt about what she had written and how I felt about her in that moment.

So, I didn't ask.

I just hugged my friend.

And she hugged me back.

Hillsboro Central/SE 3rd Ave, Day 51

Ms. Warne,

So.

So, so, so.

So many things happened yesterday after that moment in the waiting room of the Tuality Hospital. List form coming up for the sake of brevity and to help you finish reading this, as I'm sure you've got thirty others to read.

(a) Janie and I left the hospital.

(b) I asked Janie if I could have her phone number. I know, I know, Ms. Warne, that's a big, bold move for me.

(c) Janie went back to the zoo because they were having their farewell party for her and all of the other ZooTeens. She didn't want to miss the party, so she went one direction on the MAX and I went the other. My work didn't even care that I was several hours late—my boss was gone too.

(d) After work, when I got home, I asked my parents if we could have a new friend of mine come over for a while and have dinner with us.

(e) I called Janie and asked her if she'd like to come over to my house for dinner.

(f) Janie came over and my parents were very cool while she was there and after she left a couple hours later, they told me how much they liked my new friend.

And now, here I am riding home on the MAX on my next-to-the last day of my summer work.

Janie and Omar actually rode to work with me this morning as the Land Use Office was having a little party for me and my departure. Even though I'm still working tomorrow, many of the other workers are taking the day off, hence the party today.

The party was fun and I liked having Omar and Janie hang out with me. They took off, Janie to the zoo, and Omar to who-knows-where in Portland and I finished out the work day and am now on what will likely be the next to last time I ride the MAX this summer.

Since I read what Janie wrote on her laptop, we haven't really had time to talk about it much more. There is a lot I'm sure that we'll learn about each other and about ourselves as we become even better friends. I really like how easy it is, so far, to be with her.

It is comfortable, even when it's quiet.

There will be plenty of rough patches too, I'm sure. I can still hardly bring myself to dial her number on the phone and talk with her. She has already said that she would like me to call her frequently, but I still really hate talking on the phone. She even mentioned that I could learn to like texting.

One step at a time with that one, I guess.

But I'm good with it all.

Last night, she asked me before she left our house if she could read what I'd written for my summer assignment. I knew that if I shared all of this with her, I was going to be opening myself up in a vulnerable way. But then I realized that she had already done that herself, so it seemed fair. I emailed her a copy of this last night, but only after I took out the parts referring to pooped pants. I'm not yet ready to share that with her. I've got to maintain a little dignity still. When she maybe thinks of me, I want her to think of me as being me and not as someone she knows who has soiled their pants.

Who knows? Maybe someday I'll even share that with her.

And in case you're wondering how I could include in my little story what she had written word for word on her laptop, I asked her if I could use it in my assignment and she emailed it to me. I went back and put it in so you could have her words and not just my recollection of what she had written. I have her permission to include it and she said it a lot better than I ever could.

Hatfield Government Center, Day 52

"Reader . . . My tale draws to its close: . . . one brief glance at the fortunes of those whose names have most frequently recurred in this narrative, and I have done" (Chapter 38).

Ms. Warne,

Final day of the summer and for me riding the MAX. Or is it riding MAX? Sort of like "graduating from high school" or "graduating high school"—everybody thinks their way of saying it is right and the other way sounds wrong. I haven't checked, but I think I've pretty much always just used "the MAX" in my writing but it could just be "MAX" because I've started to view MAX as a living breathing entity—a "thing" that's alive and part of my life.

And even a friend.

This little summer assignment of mine has become one of those stories where one of the main characters isn't even a human.

I will see you in person next week, Ms. Warne, and I will offer up this summer assignment to be sacrificed upon the altar of your desk, ready to be dissected by your loving purple gel pen. I will also give you, as a bonus, my marked-up, annotated copy of *Jane Eyre* so you can see that I did actually read it.

You will read what has happened to me over the past few months. And you will know a little more about me and what is currently making me tick, so to speak.

I'm trying real hard not to write about Janie and myself in case you just skipped here to the end to see what happened with us. Because you will have us both in class starting next week, it will of course be clear to you how that turned out. I imagine we'll want to sit next to each other.

Since this is the last entry, it is of course necessary to wrap it all up and provide the resolution, or denouement, as you would call it.

But I don't know that there is a denouement.

My life isn't over.

And so, neither is this story. For that matter, Ms. Warne, I'm starting to think that denouement is fake—it's an illusion.

All characters—both in real life and in fiction—have so much more story to be told when the story or novel is "over." Even though Jane Eyre says that her tale is coming to its close, it's not. It's really just beginning. Again.

A new chapter, so to speak.

And that's the same with me. A new chapter.

I'm willing to take whatever grade you give me for this assignment. I've not come right out and said, "This is what I learned this summer" and I'm not going to do that here either. You're the English teacher, so you can easily figure out the theme and message and moral and all of those other literary terms that you so love to have us discuss and memorize since they'll be on the AP test next spring.

And for that matter, I don't really know if there was ever any rising action or exposition or anything else you've taught us about that stories need to have. Life, in some ways, seems to be like that. It's just been what it's been.

What I do know is this, Ms. Warne:

It's been a heck of a ride.

And I'm going over to Janie's house tonight.

To sit on the front porch with her.

I LIKE THE MAX

(to the tune of "Baby Got Back")

I like the MAX 'cause I cannot drive
The other riders all alive
When a dude get on with an all-zone pass
And a backpack for his class, we all ride.
Wanna' jump off fast cause that open door just won't last
For the biker who was riding
Or the smoker who was hiding
Oh, MAXy, I wanna' get on ya
And get to my job.
My parents they did warn me
But that long ride I got makes (me so corny)
Ooh, tough blue plastic seats
No room to sit, so I gotta' stand up
Well, take me, take me 'cause you ain't the usual train
I've watched you so far, to heck with a car
You're fast, mass, moving like a bit of the past
I'm sick of the media telling me MAXy's not the thing
Take the normal rider and he'll tell you
That MAX is hip and cool.
So, riders (yeah), riders (yeah)
Has your driver got the wheel (heck, yeah!)
Tell him, drive it, drive it, drive it, drive it, drive it
Drive that big old thang, MAXY got TRACK (repeated 4 times)

ACKNOWLEDGMENTS

Thank you: Robyn Crummer, Jessie Levine, Elizabeth Sommer, Marissa Muraoka, and the entire staff at Ooligan Press.

Thanks to the Regional Arts and Culture Council (RACC) for their encouragement and support.

Thanks to Lonny Nielsen and TriMet for their partnership and innovation.

Thanks to Kady Ferris, Paty Rincon, Shawn Cunningham, and Danielle Bylund at Multnomah County Library.

Thanks to all of the Ms. Warnes in high schools everywhere.

To the book club for their friendship and book talks.

To the Estacada High School Rangers.

To Rachel Wilczewski and Sam Barlow High School AP English, class of 20—.

To Alisha, Reevkah, Jonathan, Beckham, London, Cole, Violet, and Janice and other family members who have encouraged my writing and this book in its early drafts: my love and gratitude always.

ABOUT THE AUTHOR

Steven Christiansen is a writer and high school counselor. Originally from St. Anthony, Idaho, Steven gravitated toward books and literature from a young age and taught high school English in the Portland area for fifteen years before transitioning into a counselor role. A coming-of-age story about the power of relationships and community, *The Blue Line Letters* is the author's debut young adult fiction novel and the Multnomah County Library Writers Project 2023 choice, as well as the Distinguished Favorite of the 2024 Independent Press Award. When he's not working, Steven enjoys spending time with his wife, a playwright and director, and their four children. He loves mass transit and otters. To connect with the author, visit his website at https://www.stevenchristiansen.com.

For More Information

A teaching guide has been created for this novel by author Steven Christiansen. For more information on the guide and purchasing classroom sets of this book, please visit www.ooliganpress.com/educator-portal/.

About the Author

LAND ACKNOWLEDGMENT

We acknowledge and honor Indigenous communities—past, present, and future—whose land we currently reside on here at Portland State University. This includes the traditional and ancestral homelands of the Multnomah, Wasco, Cowlitz, Kathlamet, Clackamas, Bands of the Chinook, the Tualatin Kalapuya (Atfalati), Molalla, and many other Indigenous nations who made their homes along the Wimahl, Nch'i-Wàna, or swah'netk'qhu (all meaning "Big River or "Great River"), also known by its colonized name, the Columbia River. Descendants of these tribes are primarily members of the Confederated Tribes of Grand Ronde, Confederated Tribes of Siletz Indians, and the Chinook Nation. We acknowledge the current and long-standing oppression faced by Indigenous peoples and recognize that we are here because of the sacrifices forced upon them. We encourage everyone to find ways to support and connect with Indigenous communities and the land itself, and to remain committed to their justice and liberation. We also encourage folks to read the PSU Conflict Resolution department's Land Conflict Acknowledgement for further learning about the history of land conflict in this geographical area.

We attribute the name of our press to native peoples in Oregon. The Ooligan (also spelled Ourigan, Eulachon, or the Saak by the Tlingit peoples) is a Chinook word for a small candlefish that is abundant in the Pacific Northwest. The nutrient-rich oil produced from boiling the fish was traded between coastal and inland First Nations all along the Pacific coast, from California to Alaska, bringing prosperity and health to native communities. These routes were known as grease trails. Gradually, the L in Ooligan was replaced with an R, giving us the sound "ooregon". This usage became the name of a place and assumed its current spelling of Oregon in the course of history. We would like to honor David G. Lewis for his contributions to the press, along with his writings in the co-authored article Ourigan: Wealth of the Northwest Coast, which informed the name of our press in 2001.

We acknowledge the lack of Indigenous and people of color representation throughout the publishing industry, both in professional positions and as authors. Our press strives to publish culturally relevant titles from our local, diverse voices in order to make literature accessible and redefine who has a place within its pages. We commit to actively creating space for and uplifting Indigenous and other diverse authors through our work, including our How To: Publishing workshop and continued community partnerships.

OOLIGAN PRESS

Ooligan Press is a student-run publishing house rooted in the rich literary culture of the Pacific Northwest. Founded in 2001 as part of Portland State University's Department of English, Ooligan is dedicated to the art and craft of publishing. Students pursuing master's degrees in book publishing staff the press in an apprenticeship program under the guidance of a core faculty of publishing professionals.

Project Managers
Elizabeth Sommer
Jessie Levine
Maya Karkabi

Acquisitions
Becca Moss
Rin Kane
Angela Griffin
Emmily Tomulet

Editorial
Jessica Pelton
Marissa Muraoka
Jordan Bernard
Tanner Croom

Design
Ariana Espinoza
Marielle LeFave
Laura Renckens

Digital
Kari Olson
Madelynn Sare
Cecilia Too
Mara Palmieri

Marketing & Publicity
Rory Miner
Yomari Lobo

Online Content & DEI
AJ Adler
Jules Luck

Operations
Kara Herrera
Haley Young

Book Production
Tate Sears
Russ Johnson
Ash Murray
Nayana Silvers
Nathanial Homan
Brittany Shike
Sara Casten
Cameron Grow
Theo Thompson
Ashley Lockard
Catherine Craig
Annie Egghart
Noraa Gunn
Amber Finnegan
Isabel Lemus Kristensen